HEART OF THUNDER

Heart of Thunder
Copyright Jenny Glazebrook, 2014
Published by Jenny Glazebrook
www.jennyglazebrook.com
Gundagai, NSW

Typesetting by Book Whispers www.bookwhispers.net
Cover design created by Kremena Petrova (k_petrova84, elance).

National Library of Australia Cataloguing-in-Publication entry
Author: Glazebrook, Jenny, author.
Title: Heart of thunder / Jenny Glazebrook.
ISBN: 9780992536329 (paperback)
Series: Glazebrook, Jenny. Aussie sky ; 2
Target Audience: For young adults,
Subjects: Interpersonal conflict--Fiction.
                 Young adult fiction.
Dewey Number: A823.4

HEART OF THUNDER

Aussie Sky Series

Jenny Glazebrook

To Rev Dr Ian and Robyn Stewart,

Every young adult needs someone to teach them, encourage
them, and guide them in their walk with the Lord.
God provided you at that crucial time in my life.
As Bible college lecturers and academic teachers, you
taught me more than I knew there was to know.
As mentors, you listened and prayed for me, and lived out
an example of commitment to the Lord and His work.
As friends, you shared the joys and sorrows in my life
and encouraged me in my writing.
You have my deep love, respect and admiration.
I thank God for you from the bottom of my heart.

Chapter One

Beauty Clements scowled at the boy. He was still waiting, his hand outstretched. She narrowed her eyes. 'I'm not finished.'

His brow rose. 'How hard is it? Just write the answer.'

Beauty shook her head and flung the empty piece of paper toward him. It fluttered to the floor, and with an exasperated sigh he bent to pick it up. 'There's nothing on here.'

'That's right.'

He poked it back under her nose. 'You have to answer the question.'

Clearly he was not going to let it go. What was he, the class police? The teacher wasn't even in the room and wouldn't know if she didn't answer. She looked up to the board and re-read the question.

What can you, as a teenager, learn from art?

She knew Mr Richardson was just filling in time while he slipped out of the room. So why should she bother answering such a ridiculous question? She already knew she hated staring at other people's squiggles and brushstrokes. She didn't even want to go on next week's excursion to the city art gallery. Sitting in a bus being annoyed by rowdy, excited classmates was not her idea of fun. All she wanted was to be out in the fresh air, riding her horse and enjoying real life. If the artists all painted like her brother Blaze, that would different. Blaze had once won a prize for his portrait of her twin brother, Storm. Storm had been sitting atop his horse, dressed in his circus outfit and looking down at everyone with his usual lofty disdain. Lucky Storm. He had left school and was working on the roads. If only she could find a job she could leave this zoo as well. She wouldn't call it a circus. It didn't deserve such a compliment.

'Hey, circus girl, hurry up.'

Beauty didn't even bother answering as she sat back. The boy dropped the notepaper onto her desk. 'I'm talking to you, girl.'

Girl? What was wrong with him? She had a name, not that she liked it, but he might as well use it. A tall girl stood and came to stand before her. Great. Another one to join in the fray. As expected, the whole class was now listening, interested to see what developed. Why disappoint them? They were wanting another fight from the 'ex-circus girl'. She would give it to them.

'Hey, Beauty, he's talking to you.' The tall girl now glowered down at her. Funny, she didn't feel threatened. Maybe if she cared what they thought she would. But the truth was she didn't care about anything since she'd left the circus. Anything but Montford Express – her horse, her best friend in the world.

The girl flipped Beauty's ruler off the desk. 'I said he was talking to you.'

Beauty looked up, eyes narrowed. 'Really? I didn't hear my name.'

'Which one? Is it really Beauty, because we're thinking it should be "Beast."'

She heard the sniggers. Slowly, she stood. 'Or cat. Don't forget you all call me the cat. Cats have exceptional hearing, you know. And intelligence. Oh, and don't underestimate the sharp claws. I'm not stupid. I know what you call me.'

The tall girl towered over Beauty, but she held her own. Like Storm, she had her lofty expression perfected. Her half smile and cold eyes could make anybody back away. But her next move shocked them all. In a split second she had leapt to the top of the desk. Hands on hips, she studied the tall girl for a fraction of a second before turning around and doing a backflip that had her soaring over the girl's head and landing perfectly on the desk behind.

She heard the disbelieving gasps. Until now she had refused to perform for any of them. But now, why not? In fact, why not give them the full performance? Storm would love it if he were there. He would probably join in. She poised herself for more action.

'Beauty Clements!'

The loud, deep voice had students scurrying back to their seats. Beauty looked to Mr Richardson standing in the doorway, his expression one of disbelief.

'Yes, sir?'

'What do you think you are doing?'

Beauty saw the humour in the situation for the first time. The teacher had left the classroom for only a few minutes and this is what he returned to. One of his students standing on a desk, poised to backflip. The teacher's desk had been her next target; that much was obvious from a glance.

Beauty began to giggle. The giggle transformed into a laugh and the relief of it was immense. She hadn't laughed for a very long time. She didn't even know why it was all so funny. She was sure she was in big trouble. The students hated her and called her 'the cat' behind her back. She and her brothers and sisters had been forced to leave the circus to focus on their education, but now only she was left being educated in this narrow minded school. Blaze had left home first, followed closely by the triplets. Misty was enjoying a job training horses while Prince and Starre were at Uni, enjoying a life where they could make their own choices. And Storm, her twin, her one ally, had managed to convince their father he would be better off working. She alone was left here, misunderstood and a misfit. What was so funny about that? She had no idea, but her laughter rang out until even the teacher had to smile. The students weren't so amused.

'She's crazy.'

'What is wrong with her?'

She heard the comments around her, but still she laughed. Alone in the world, completely misunderstood, miserable and lost. Really, what else could she do but laugh?

Hundreds of kilometres away from Everdeen high school and its art class, Mayor Thomas Eldwin moved through the city art gallery, gazing intently at each picture. Though balding and grey, his eyes held the enthusiasm of a child in a toy shop.

'That's good.' He pointed to a lifelike bush scene.

The judge beside him raised his eyebrows in surprise. 'You're quite perceptive considering you've never studied art. However, the theme is too common.'

Mr Eldwin smiled. 'You're the judge, so you ought to know, but I think it's the common things that make our life worth living.'

The judge shrugged as he moved the mayor toward the next section of the gallery. 'True enough. But I think I've seen enough common things in my life to appreciate what is different.'

Mr Eldwin wasn't listening. He was reading the bold announcement pinned above the entrance to the next section: 'Section Five. Theme: Love. 'I hope there's nothing pornographic in here.'

The judge shook his head, smiling politely at the joke. 'This is a public display. We are very selective.'

Mr Eldwin nodded absently. He was glancing at all the paintings with the 'Love' theme. Mothers with children, couples on picnics, weddings …

He stopped in front of a painting which stood out from the rest. He caught his breath in a gasp, then stared as he absorbed the thousand words spoken by the picture. For a few moments he couldn't speak. Then he found his voice. 'I don't much like the religious theme in this one.' He swallowed hard, pulling himself together. 'It's a bit too, well …'

'Overwhelming?'

'Yes. It's kind of morbid or something.'

'I agree, but I'm not supposed to be judging the theme. I'm judging the skill of the artist and the idea, and this one's good.'

'It is?'

'Very. I've never seen a painting which has caused as much reaction as this one. It's hard hitting. The artist knew what he was doing and not one stroke of his brush was by chance.'

'Who was the artist?' Mr Eldwin squinted as he searched for a name on the canvas.

The judge pointed to a small signature in the corner of the painting. 'Blaze Clements. He's young, apparently, but talented.'

'Blaze?' Mr Eldwin's eyes became alight with respect. 'Blaze Clements, the trainee minister?'

'That would make sense, given the message of his work. I guess he's one and the same. How many people have a name like Blaze?'

'Good point. I don't know what the parents were doing, naming those kids after horses.'

The judge was now watching the mayor with interest. 'So you know him?'

Mr Eldwin looked away, refusing to meet the judge's eyes. 'Not very well. He leads the church youth group my son attends.'

'So your son is religious but you're not?'

'Well, it was kind of my fault he got into religion.' Mr Eldwin looked shamefaced at the admission. 'I used to take him to Sunday school and went to church myself sometimes. That was before I realised God doesn't exist. I guess Chappy – my son – just never grew out of the belief.' He heaved a deep sigh. 'He's at Blaze's place right now, and no doubt I'll be subjected to another sermon full of Blaze's ideas about God when he gets home.'

The judge turned back to the painting and his voice was low and thoughtful. 'If this Blaze fellow were to grow out of his belief, he could make millions. It's deep. In fact, it's the best I've seen in a long time.'

Mr Eldwin laughed as he shook his head, refusing to look back at the painting. 'Blaze is not the type to care about money.' With that, he turned to comment on another painting, neatly closing the subject. From the day he lost his younger son, he had determined never to think of God again. No small feat when his other son continued to hold to his belief that God did indeed exist, and in fact, could bring good from suffering.

***

Chappy Eldwin stood in the middle of Blaze's lounge room, the centre of attention, as usual. Nothing could keep him away from the Bible studies Blaze led. It was here that he found a sense of purpose and belonging in life; it was here he was able to put aside the pain of losing his little brother and focus on the God who claimed he had a purpose in everything.

Once again Chappy's teenage heart was churning but he shut it out. He forced his cheeky, spontaneous smile. 'Come on, guys, move over.' He stood poised, ready to dive onto Blaze's three-seater lounge. 'You'd better move right now 'cause I'm coming in.'

The teenage girls who were stretched across the chair squealed and jumped out of the way just before he landed right in the middle of the cushions. Chappy grinned at them and patted the spaces beside him. 'Okay, you can come back now. There's room for you as well.'

The girls glared at him, while Chappy beckoned to some other members of the group. 'Come on, guys. There's room for you, too.'

The rest of the teenagers filling the lounge room responded to his signal and soon there were at least five bodies piled on the lounge, pushing and shoving one another.

Chappy called out over his shoulder. 'Okay, Blaze. We're ready to begin the study.'

Blaze came from the kitchen and studied the scene before him. Slowly his face lit into a smile, and his dark eyes began to dance. 'Do you really think you can concentrate like that?'

'Of course.' Chappy threw Blaze a cheeky grin. One of the teenagers beneath the pile of bodies managed to squeeze free, more squashed than annoyed. 'Especially now. We can even fit another one. Come on, Bonnie.'

Chappy beckoned to an attractive twenty year old sitting across the room. She chuckled as her sparkling blue eyes took in the lounge chair piled with wriggling teenage bodies. 'Don't even think about it, Chappy. I'm quite comfortable here, thanks.'

'Why not?' Chappy put on a hurt look. 'Don't tell me you're going all adult on us.'

Bonnie let out a laugh. 'I am an adult.'

'I thought you were still like us at heart.'

She shook her head, her eyes twinkling with merriment. 'I've never been like you at heart, Chappy Eldwin. Even as a teenager I was a little bit responsible.'

Chappy immediately turned back to Blaze, who still stood in the kitchen doorway. 'Is that true? Was she really responsible as a teenager?'

Everyone watched as Blaze leaned against the doorway, his expression becoming tender with memories. 'I can't say.'

'Come on!' Chappy wriggled like an excited little boy. 'You can't keep secrets like that from us.'

Blaze shrugged and laughed. 'I honestly can't say. How exactly do you define responsible?'

Bonnie laughed triumphantly at Chappy, shooting a grateful look in Blaze's direction. 'Good point. You can't judge how responsible someone is unless you understand what it means to be responsible. Which means, Chappy Eldwin, you have no hope of making an accurate judgement. As you always say, takes one to know one.'

Chappy couldn't help laughing, knowing that, once again, Bonnie Blake had beaten him at his own game. She always outwitted him but he didn't mind. She was a lot of fun.

***

A few streets away, a silent figure stood in the shadows, watching Mr Eldwin lock the door of the art gallery and head to his car. The display of art would be viewed in the morning and the mayor would once more gain the approval of the people and make money to fight child abuse. Or maybe not. The figure moved out of the shadows and carefully chose a rock. He flung with all his might and cringed at the loud shattering of glass. He glanced around. Silence. It seemed nobody had heard. With youthful agility, he climbed through the window of the dark gallery and set to work. The light from the street lamp shone toward the section furthest from the window and the youth decided he would get to it last. Pulling a knife from his pocket he began his work, violently slashing at every framed picture he could feel in front of him. He had vandalised five when he stopped and looked around the room. If only he could see what he was destroying. That would be a lot more satisfying.

With renewed courage, he headed toward the light. What he saw made him stop short. The light from the street lamp shone directly onto a picture that matched the destruction in his own heart. There, in the section under the theme of love, was a painting of a paddock full of mutilated sheep and lambs. A wolf stood looking over the carnage, a wicked gleam in his eye as he licked the blood from his mouth.

'Someone's got a sick sense of humour,' the youth muttered, planning to leave the painting intact. That is, until he looked closer at the edge of the painting, shadowed by a chair across the hall. There in the shadow sat a shepherd in flowing white robes covered in blood. His arms, legs and face were torn and bleeding. His condition was worse than that of the mutilated sheep surrounding him. But sheltered under his arm was a snowy white lamb that had been protected from the wolf.

The youth couldn't suppress a gasp as he shook his head at the powerful image. Then anger toward the person who had portrayed something so idealistic overwhelmed him. 'Nobody protected me!' He shouted as he cursed and swore, slashing at the painting. Looking at the tattered canvas before him, he slumped into an exhausted heap. Reaching a hand to his face, he was horrified to find traces of tears on his cheeks. He had not cried in years; tears were a sign of weakness. If he was to survive, he needed to be in control. Blindly, he rushed from the room.

CHAPTER TWO

As the group broke up and went home, Blaze kept his eye on Bonnie. He watched as she smiled and laughed with the teenagers, her blue eyes shining with life and a serene maturity beyond her years. She was intriguing. She was so comfortable with every member of the youth group, but when she was alone with him, she seemed devoid of all confidence. Her fingers would reach nervously to the scars on her hands and arms and her brilliant blue eyes would avoid him.

He admired those eyes now, as she stood just outside his door, making conversation with the teenagers as they headed home. His mind began planning the portrait he would paint of her. It would be a picture of true, inner joy. He would paint her just as she was, physical blemishes and all, but he would capture the inward beauty etched in her expression so everyone would know her scars were insignificant. Tenderly, he allowed his eyes to follow every curve of her face.

Finally, the last of the group had gone and Blaze was left alone with Bonnie. She smiled shyly under his scrutiny as he came and stood on the doorstep below her. His eyes were now level with hers. Blaze noted the way she made an effort to look directly at him. 'Well, I guess I'd better go home, too.'

Blaze nodded, unable to keep the tenderness from his expression.

She cleared her throat. 'It went well tonight.'

Again he nodded and she gave a nervous laugh. 'What are you thinking?'

He reached for her scarred fingers and noticed the way her eyes widened then clouded with confusion. He touched the skin so wrinkled from the burns. His hand tightened on hers as he drew her closer to him. 'I'm thinking you're beautiful.'

She blushed as she avoided his dark eyes. She did that whenever he revealed the intensity of his feelings for her.

'I mean that.' He tilted his head to touch her lips gently with his own. She responded with warmth and enthusiasm and he knew that it was not disinterest that made her keep her eyes away. How long would it take her to believe he truly did love her just as she was? He longed for her to be comfortable with him the way she had been so many years ago: the way she was before her accident. The day she had run into burning stables to save his family's horses had changed their lives. The extensive burns to her body had taken away her love of life for a long time and Blaze had wondered if she would ever recover. He was so grateful God had reached out to her and made sense of the pain when no one else could. She now understood God's love for her, but would she ever understand his?

***

Blaze awoke to the sound of his phone. Who would call him so early in the morning? It was his day off and he had planned to sleep in. He'd better answer it. It could be one of his family members in trouble.

'Blaze Clements speaking.'

'Blaze, Mayor Thomas Eldwin here. I'm sorry to be the bearer of bad news.'

Blaze's heart beat faster. Surely something hadn't happened to the likeable Chappy?

'It's about your painting and, well …'

A myriad of emotions rushed through Blaze in the time it took Mr Eldwin to pause. First relief that Chappy was okay, then concern. Had his painting been rejected from the display because of its controversial nature? Mr Eldwin had made it clear on previous occasions that he did not hold the same religious interests as his son.

'Yes?' Blaze tried to keep the apprehension from his voice.

'Well, we had a break in at the gallery last night. I'm afraid your painting has been destroyed.'

Disappointment overwhelmed him. He had put his heart and soul into that painting. He had believed God would use it to have a powerful impact on many people.

'It wasn't just yours. Many have been destroyed,' Mr Eldwin added.

'Does anyone know who did it?'

'We have an idea. But don't worry, you will still receive your prize money. Your painting won first prize.'

Blaze hung his head. The prize money meant nothing compared with having people see the painting and be moved by the love of God. He couldn't prevent the sigh that escaped. 'Put the prize money into your fund to prevent child abuse. We might as well make something good come from this.'

The mayor remained quiet and Blaze felt the need to fill the silence. 'Thanks for letting me know, Mr Eldwin.'

'I really am sorry, Blaze,' Mr Eldwin managed just before Blaze hung up.

***

Bonnie sat in her university lecture, unable to concentrate. Blaze's words were plaguing her mind. He thought she was beautiful, scars and all. So why couldn't she see herself that way?

'Why God?' The question filled her mind again. 'Will I ever get used to the way I am?' Her silent conversations with God often ran along the same lines. She could see that her pain had turned her to God, but now that she knew Him, why did she still struggle with the way she looked? She didn't regret saving the horses, but could she have done it without risking her own life? She remembered Beauty's face as she stood screaming, begging her to do something as the flames roared through the stables. If she had a choice, she knew she would do it again, but that didn't make it any easier to live with the scars. She frowned, rubbing the wrinkled hands that still itched unbearably at times. She felt so free when she wasn't thinking of them. She could be herself, but then she would look at Blaze and feel inadequate. He seemed perfect in every way. She had never dreamed such a man could love her. She loved his tall, dark looks and athletic build. She loved the depth of his eyes and his thoughtful nature. He could be so serious at times, but it didn't take much to make him laugh or smile. She loved the way he cared for his younger brothers and sisters, even though he had left home. Most of all, she loved the way he was so in touch with God.

She shook her head. *He never seems to make a mistake, but he must sometimes. After all, he is only human.*

That very evening she saw Blaze was indeed human and his understanding of God was not complete. He was pacing the room as he told her about the vandal who had destroyed his ark work.

'Sometimes I just don't understand how God works.' He sat down beside her on the lounge, but she could see how restless and confused he still felt. 'I really believe God inspired the idea for that painting. Every step of the way I knew it was something special, but now?'

Bonnie nodded, her heart constricting. Unable to help herself, she reached out and put her arms around him, drawing him close. He was usually the one who initiated contact, but his unexpected vulnerability overcame her feelings of inadequacy.

'I don't understand either.' She rested her head on his shoulder. 'But I believe all your paintings are inspired by God. Even if they touch the heart of just one person, they're worth it.'

Blaze nodded and sighed as he leaned into her embrace. 'You're right. But that painting didn't even get to be seen.'

'Yes it did.' Bonnie sat up, her bright eyes burning into his. 'Mr Eldwin saw it. The judge must have seen it for you to get first prize. I saw it and so did most of the youth group. And I know it sounds crazy, but maybe it had some impact on whoever destroyed it.'

'The vandal destroyed it in the dark, and it wasn't just mine. The attack was random.' Despite Blaze's words, Bonnie could see his mood was beginning to lighten. Suddenly he squeezed her tight. 'You're right, Bonnie. God did allow some people to see the painting. I just have to trust. Who knows what good he will bring from this?'

***

In his small flat a troubled youth lay in his bed feeling dissatisfied with his work of the previous night. The pleasure he had gained in the past from venting his anger and destroying beauty was a long time in coming.

'It's because that painting was a picture of destruction,' he told himself. 'It showed mutilation and violence. I should have left it alone.'

He fingered the blade on his pocket knife and felt a measure of regret. The knife still had a few small remnants of the canvas clinging to the blade. He flicked them away and watched them drop to the floor. His mind wandered to the story he had heard years ago in Sunday school about Jesus being the good shepherd and dying on the cross.

'What a bloodthirsty story those Christians cling to.' He let out a harsh laugh. 'And they claim it's about love!'

He turned and faced the wall, willing sleep to come, but his mind and his eyes remained wide open. The image haunted him, filling his head, challenging him. The shepherd and the sheep swam into focus and he could even see the muscles and the sinews beneath the skin of the strong arms holding the lamb like a precious treasure. The shepherd's eyes were calm and steady, and his countenance was powerful, yet gentle. The character etched in the lines of his face was unforgettable.

Love, he thought and sat up. That's what it is. Love. That man looks at the wolf and says 'You can fight, but you won't win. This one is mine.'

A knife-like pain twisted in his gut. 'I've never been loved that

that,' he said bitterly. 'If I had been loved like that I wouldn't be where I am today.'

He shook his head to rid himself of the painful memories and bent down to pick up one of the scraps of canvas.

'Blaze.' He read the word and wondered what it meant. Another word which signified destruction? How could someone who could depict suffering and violence so effectively have given their work such a holy, religious theme?

'He's a psycho,' he told himself and shut his eyes, willing the image to go away. When it lingered, he turned again to the bottle of alcohol by his bed.

Chapter Three

Beauty Clements stared at her father. Had she really heard right? Did he really just say he had asked his girlfriend to come and live with them?

He shuffled, looking unsure for the first time. 'Whatever you say, Noreen is coming, Beauty. We have plenty of spare rooms now Blaze and the triplets have moved out.'

His words provoked her, lighting an angry, thunderous fire in her heart. He said it so calmly, as though it was the most normal thing in the world. So this was it. No questioning whether she minded a strange woman replacing her mother; no asking her feelings about it. She refused to look at him, but he didn't seem to care. It was as though he was immune to her outbursts now.

She gritted her teeth, seething. 'How could you?'

He turned his back, not even looking at her. 'Beauty, why do you always have to be the difficult one? I thought having twins would be easy after triplets but you and Storm ...' He let the words hang.

The angry words she had been ready to spit out died on her lips. Why did her father always make out everything was her fault? Of course her older siblings had been easier. Her mother had been there. No one had counted on her mother losing her life while giving birth to her. Storm had arrived quickly and easily. She had been the difficult one. Always her.

At her silence, her father turned back and a satisfied smile filled his face. 'It will be good for you to have a mother around again.

Maybe she can sort you out.'

A tempest rose inside her, filling her with all consuming anger. She let out a scream that began somewhere in the pit of her stomach and rose up into her throat. 'A mother? I don't even have a proper father. You have no idea what would be good for me, do you? Well, I didn't ask to kill Mum. I didn't even ask to be born!'

The shrill ring of her father's phone filled the empty silence following her outburst. Her father reached for it and Beauty knew the conversation was over in his thinking. She ran to her room and slammed the door shut, knowing she had to get away before she did something terrible. Right now she honestly hated her father so much she could drive a knife right through him.

She knew it was Blaze on the phone. He always rang on Thursday nights to see how the family were going, but she was too worked up to talk to him tonight. Although Blaze had left home almost three years ago, he believed they still needed him, and though she would never admit it, he was right. Their father was preoccupied with his own life and didn't know how to offer guidance to lost, hurting teenagers. From the day she was born, the same day her mother died, her older brother had been the only real parent figure she had.

Through the locked door, Beauty listened as her father went to get Storm from his room. Had he told Storm about Noreen? Storm probably wouldn't even care. She could hear parts of Storm's heated conversation with Blaze. Storm's 'don't care' attitude and heartless, gruff comments always grated on the rest of the family and only Blaze seemed able to keep calm. She knew the anger was one-sided.

'Beauty, your turn.'

She ignored her father's bellowing voice. Didn't he even know how upset she still was? The man was clueless.

'Beauty, come and talk with your brother. Let him talk some sense into you.'

Beauty let out a breath of disgust. As if that would encourage her to talk to Blaze. The truth was she wanted to talk to him, but not with her father around.

She heard her father walk across the room. 'Me again, Blaze. I've put you on speaker phone. She can hear you, so say your piece. But I warn you, she's in a mood.'

Her father was bellowing as usual.

She heard Blaze chuckle. 'So is Storm. I don't really want to deal with his angry twin. Tell Beauty I'll catch up with her next week.'

'No, no, I'd like you to talk to her.'

A tinge of frustration crept into Blaze's voice. 'Okay. What's upsetting her?'

Beauty cringed as his father let out a carefree laugh. 'Who'd know? Puberty, no doubt.'

That was the final straw. Beauty saw red. She picked up the thing nearest her – a framed sketch Blaze had done of her horse, Montford Express – and threw it against the wall. Glass shattered and she knew Blaze would have heard it.

'Tell her I'll catch her next week.' Blaze's voice came out sounding tired and sad. Beauty was glad he hadn't seen what she had broken. She moved slowly across the room and knelt on the floor. The glass had scratched the paper and the picture was destroyed. Just like her heart. Even Blaze hadn't made time for her tonight. He probably had a date with his beloved Bonnie.

Beauty's hand tightened around the remains of the picture of Montford Express until she had screwed it up into a tight ball.

Remembering how her father had so easily put her anger down to puberty, Beauty's face darkened again. She threw the scrunched up sketch across the room and stormed from the house, wanting to escape but knowing she could never really could. Not from herself.

* * *

Bonnie could tell Blaze was concerned. She put a hand on his arm. 'Did something happen when you called your family?'

Blaze's eyes shot to hers. 'Oh, sorry Bonnie. Yes, but that's okay. This night is about us. I don't want my family interfering with our time together.'

She smiled. 'But they are a part of you, Blaze. And I want to know. I love them too.'

Blaze shook his head. 'I know, but this is our time. Just you and me. Let's talk about –'

He stopped as a flash of lightning streaked across the city skyline.

'About Beauty's moods?' Bonnie grinned. 'That's what the lightning reminds me of anyway.'

Blaze chuckled and drew her to his side. 'Can't escape it anywhere, can I?' He looked up into the darkening sky. 'I think we might get wet.'

She snuggled closer to him as they walked. 'That's okay. So what do you want to talk about?'

'About youth group. I think I have the answer to the concentration problem and it involves you.' Blaze's expression was thoughtful and Bonnie waited. 'I think we should divide them. Maybe you can take the girls and I'll take the boys.'

A smile formed on Bonnie's face and Blaze stopped. 'What?'

'Handing the girls over to me? What's the problem, Blaze? You can't handle the girls' little tiffs anymore? I thought you were an expert, you know, with all that practice calming down Beauty and all.'

Blaze chuckled. 'You know that's not it. I just think the group is getting too big, and some most teenagers are distracted by the opposite gender being in the same room.'

Bonnie was thoughtful. 'I agree, but separating them might turn some away.'

'It might, but are they there for the right reason if they are so interested in the opposite sex?'

Bonnie grinned at him. 'Does it matter? It certainly didn't hurt me to be interested in a certain handsome teenager when I was searching for God.'

Blaze smiled back. 'Really? So was your interest of any value in the end?'

Bonnie pretended to think, but Blaze turned her to face him

and kissed her tenderly before she had a chance to respond. When he stepped back, his eyes were filled with concern. 'You're soaked through.'

'So are you.' She felt the shoulders of his jacket, then jumped at a loud crack of thunder. She saw that Blaze was about to laugh at her edginess, but then it caught in his throat as his eyes focussed on something. She followed his gaze. A few metres away, someone lay on the ground, moaning. Blaze raced over first and crouched over the curled up figure, shaking him gently. 'Can you hear me? Are you okay?'

The person moaned again, and as he turned his head, a bright flash of lightning revealed a teenager with bloodshot eyes.

'He's drunk.' Blaze fell to his knees and tried to roll the teenager over. 'What's your name?'

The teenager slurred something incomprehensible, every syllable an effort.

'Where do you live?' Blaze tried again.

The youth tried unsuccessfully to get up, his face contorted as he looked into the concerned dark eyes above him.

Blaze turned to Bonnie, 'Can you bring the car? I'll take him home and get him out of the cold. Then maybe I can find out who he is.'

Bonnie nodded, taking the car keys from Blaze's hand. In a few minutes she returned and then helped Blaze struggle to get the drunk teenager into the vehicle. To her dismay, he was sick as soon as they sat him in the back seat and a foul stench filled the car. Blaze ignored it and instead concentrated on getting the teenager comfortable. The teenager slumped into the seat and Blaze struggled to get the seat belt on him. He frowned deeply as he glanced up at Bonnie. 'I should see if he has a wallet on him, then I can find out who he is. His parents are probably worried sick.'

Yes, sick was an appropriate word right now. Sick was the only thing Bonnie could think about with the mess on the back seat and the stench that made her want to gag. She managed to nod at Blaze.

'I'll get him into some dry clothes first.'

Trust Blaze to be willing to give up his clothes for a drunk.

Bonnie climbed into the front passenger seat and wound down a window, ignoring the rain drops splashing her face and arms. She needed fresh air.

Blaze glanced worriedly at his back seat passenger, then at Bonnie. 'Let's get him home and cleaned up.'

'And I'll clean out the car.' She knew it would be an unpleasant job, but if Blaze could clean up the teenager, then surely that was the least she could do. It was worth the offer to have Blaze smile at her the way he was now; like she was amazing and like he had never met anyone like her before in his life.

She smiled in return, forgetting to be uncomfortable as she soaked up the tenderness in his eyes.

***

Riding her magnificent white horse, Beauty felt less alone than she had all day. People made her feel inadequate and lost. Being outside in the fresh country air with Montford Express gave her a freedom she couldn't find anywhere else. She glanced up at the storm clouds overhead, thinking how quickly the darkness had settled in.

She patted Montford's neck and continued talking to him. 'I hate school. I just can't get the hang of Maths.' She strained her eyes to see the muddy track they were following. 'I don't see why I need it, anyway. And they're all snobs at Everdeen. They call me "The Cat" behind my back. I've heard them.'

She fell silent, thinking about her situation and trying to force the recent conversation with her father from her mind. She felt the horse beneath her hesitate, but was too busy trying to calm her own disturbed emotions to take much notice. She gave him another reassuring pat. 'Keep going, Montford Express.' There was nothing else they could do, really. It was no use straining to see through the dark and rain, trying to find a faster way home.

The bushland around her was thinning slightly, but Beauty discounted her horse's skittishness. The sound of the thunder blocked out any other sounds for a few moments, and all too late

Beauty heard a car's motor and blinked as light glared into her eyes and the ground beneath the horses hooves became hard.

In an instant she knew. They had stepped out of the bush and onto the main road. There was a terrific thud as Montford let cut a screaming whinny of terror and pain. Lights flashed before Beauty's eyes. She felt herself thrown and tried to focus. Everything was blurry and there was an eerie feeling in the air. A moment ago there had been so much noise and now it was deadly quiet.

She strained her eyes before she saw a car – a twisted, upside down wreck of a car. Other vehicles had come along the road and stopped and people were rushing in all directions. And there by her side lay Montford Express, lifeless.

'Monty!' Her voice came out hoarse. He didn't stir.

'Montford Express,' she called again, lifting her head to look around.

'It's too late,' said a voice a long way off. It came from somewhere over near the upside down car where another vehicle had now stopped. She knelt in a crumpled heap on the ground and buried her head in her arms. They weren't talking about Monty. Someone else had died. Someone in the car. And it was all her fault. She could hear voices but they all seemed to blur. Then she heard a man shout out as he rushed toward her. 'There's a girl over here! And a horse ' He bent down and gently pushed the dark, tangled hair from her face 'It's okay, love. An ambulance is on the way.'

Beauty just stared at him, unable to comprehend what was happening. She began to shake, oblivious to the sirens, the flashing lights, the emergency workers. It wasn't until an ambulance officer came to her side and tried to move her that she came to life. She ran to her horse and clung to his lifeless body.

'I killed you!' she cried out brokenly. 'I'm so sorry. Oh, Monty, what have I done? I can't live in this horrible world without you.'

She wished she could cry and let out this awful, twisted pain inside her, but no tears came. Instead, the rain continued to weep on her behalf.

Chapter Four

Bonnie returned to find Blaze pacing the room, studying the teenager's wallet. She knew her hair was dishevelled and she couldn't get rid of the unpleasant odour from her hands, no matter how much she washed them. 'So did you find any ID in there?'

Blaze stopped his pacing and turned, holding up the wallet. 'Yes. This was in his back pocket. His name is Derek Sheen.' He frowned toward the drunken teenager, now fast asleep on the lounge. He was dressed in a pair of Blaze's old jeans and t-shirt. They were too big, but they were clean. 'I know I've heard the name before but I can't remember where.'

'So what now?'

Blaze drew in a deep breath. 'Well, I could try to find the boy's parents but that might cause trouble. But then, maybe they need to know what their son is doing out on the streets late at night.'

Bonnie nodded and lifted a hand toward her face before catching a whiff of her own smell again. She shoved her hands in her pockets. 'I think you should call Mr Mathison.'

Blaze frowned. 'I thought of that, but it's late. And I don't want our minister thinking I palm off all the difficult cases to him.'

Bonnie smiled as she came to Blaze's side. 'I don't think the title of youth pastor means you have to know exactly what to do in every situation, Blaze Clements. After all, you were trained to teach and counsel the young people of the church, not to reach out to drunken teenagers who probably aren't even sure what a Bible is.'

Blaze smiled at her argument, gave her a quick hug, then screwed up his nose. 'I'll ring Mr Mathison, my little counsellor, but I think you'd better get home and out of those sick smelling clothes.'

Bonnie sighed and Blaze reached for her, tenderly placing his hands either side of her face. He gazed deep into her eyes. 'I know. I wish you didn't have to go, too. One day we won't have to count the hours until we see each other again.'

Bonnie drew in a breath. 'Five o'clock tomorrow seems a long time away.'

He simply nodded and drew her into his arms. She pushed back. 'Blaze, it's okay. I know I smell bad.'

He grinned and pulled her close. 'I know, but I have to hold you one more time anyway.'

She smiled in contentment and allowed herself to snuggle into the comfort of his embrace. Then she pulled back again. 'Maybe you can put up with it, but I can't stand the smell of myself. I'll see you tomorrow, Blaze.'

He let her go. 'Till tomorrow then. And may you come back smelling sweeter than a rose.'

She screwed up her nose at him and laughed. 'Yes, may I do that!'

***

Throughout the next day's lectures, Bonnie thought little of her nursing studies and a great deal about Blaze and his compassion toward the teenager. He was such an amazing, godly young man. She felt so inadequate; so undeserving of him.

She was surprised to see his car in the driveway as she arrived home late in the afternoon. She raced into the lounge room, knowing he would be there chatting with her mother. He was. She couldn't help smiling at the sight of him. 'What happened with Derek?'

Blaze jumped up from the chair, eyes sparkling. 'Not even a "hello, I've missed you"?'

Her mother made a tactful exit and Bonnie grinned. 'I'm sorry.

Will this do?' She ran and threw her arms around him.

'Almost.' He kissed her, then gave a satisfied smile. 'That's more like what I was after!'

Bonnie blushed, forgetting about Derek for a few moments as he held her close then led her to the lounge. She settled beside him. 'So what happened?'

'With Derek? Mr Mathison knows him. Apparently he's had a drinking problem since he was about ten. He lives with his father, who incidentally, is hardly ever there. Anyway, Mr Mathison took him home. I rang this morning, before Derek went to school, and he thanked me for helping him and asked to come and meet me.'

Bonnie's eyes lit up. 'You might be able to help him.'

Blaze was shaking his head. 'Mr Mathison has tried several times. Derek is one of those teenagers who always says he wants help, but doesn't want to help himself. I'll be a friend to Derek, but I'll have to set boundaries or every second of every day will be tied up with him.'

Bonnie nodded. Blaze took both her hands in his, his expression turning serious. 'Bonnie, I also got a call from Dad this afternoon.'

His tone scared her. Blaze always rang his father; his father never rang him. 'Is everything okay?'

The sorrow in his eyes gave her the answer before he spoke. 'Beauty had an accident last night. She and Montford Express were hit by a car and Montford was killed.'

Bonnie gasped, horrified. Poor Beauty. And poor Montford. Tears filled her eyes. That horse had meant everything to Blaze's youngest sister.

'Beauty's not badly hurt,' Blaze said. 'Well, physically, anyway. But a little boy was killed in the car that hit her. Dad has tried to talk to her but she won't come out of her room. She refuses to eat or go to school and Dad can't work out what to do. He asked if she can come and live with me for a while.'

Bonnie listened to Blaze, a pain building somewhere deep in her chest. She could see in Blaze's expression how much he felt for his sister and her heart ached for him. 'You know, this could be what turns her to God.'

Blaze gave her a questioning look and she smiled sadly.

'Don't you remember how it was for me? That carefree, haphazard teenager who had no time for God until she nearly lost her life in a fire?'

He reached to wipe one of her tears. 'You could be right.'

Bonnie took his hand and squeezed it. 'Let's pray for Beauty.'

Blaze nodded and bowed his head. Together they asked God to heal Beauty Clements and show them the best way to handle the situation. Then with heartfelt pleas, Blaze prayed for the family of the little boy, and asked God to bring Beauty's heart to a point where she would accept God's love for her.

Chapter Five

It was a silent, subdued teenager who moved in with Blaze Clements a few days later. She allowed her brother to take her suitcase, but turned away when he attempted to give her a hug. She ignored Bonnie, and her short, terse answers made it clear she wanted to be left to herself.

'I can't get her to talk.' Johnny huffed out a sigh when Beauty shut the door to her new room. 'I'm hoping you and Bonnie can do something for her.'

Blaze nodded and silently asked God for wisdom in dealing with his difficult sister.

'She probably just needs time.' The words reassured his father, but Blaze wished he could believe them himself. His father put a hand on his shoulder.

'Noreen and I are so grateful. She wasn't game to move in while Beauty was around. Who knows what would have happened.'

Frustration rose within Blaze, but he kept silent. Why couldn't his father look beyond himself and his relief that he could now invite Noreen to move in with him?

He didn't even say goodbye to Beauty, and his sigh of relief as he left was loud and heartfelt. Blaze shook his head. Okay, so now his father was free to live without Beauty's constant criticism and anger. But what about him? What was he supposed to do with his troubled little sister? He let out a long breath. 'Lord, help me, please.'

It took several minutes to gather the courage to approach

Beauty's room. He had no idea what to expect. Would she be angrily throwing her clothes from her suitcase into one of the cupboards or lying face down on the bed, sobbing her heart out? He thought her anger would be easier for him to bear.

She didn't respond when he knocked, so after hesitating a few moments, he walked away. He would let her decide when she was ready to come out.

It was nearly an hour before Beauty came out of her room. She approached the table where Bonnie and Blaze sat expectantly. She tossed her long dark hair as she gave her brother a cold glare, ignoring Bonnie. Blaze held his breath. He wondered if she would say anything about the painting he had put on the wall of her room. He had spent most of the last two days painting Montford Express from memory. He didn't know if it would help Beauty or cause her more pain. Whatever the result, he had needed to do it for himself. Montford Express had been Beauty's circus horse and a part of their family from the time Beauty was eighteen months old. Despite her dry eyes, Beauty had to be in anguish right now.

But her eyes bored coldly into his. 'You got the legs wrong.'

Blaze raised an eyebrow. 'I did?'

She gave him a look of disgust. 'He's mostly white, Blaze. You've put way too much black on his legs. And his coat isn't shiny enough.'

Blaze noticed her use of the present tense and realised she hadn't yet accepted that Montford was gone. He quashed the defence that sprang to mind and made himself smile. 'I'm happy to fix it for you.'

She shook her head and her hands went to her hips. 'Don't bother. You'd just get it wrong again.'

Blaze swallowed hard, reminding himself she was hurting. 'Okay. Well, feel free to help yourself to my paints and do it yourself if you like.'

She turned as though about to leave, but Blaze pulled out a chair for her. 'Beauty, we need to talk.' He pretended not to notice her challenging attitude, though he could see Bonnie suppressing a smile. Although beautiful, Beauty was fierce.

She plopped herself into the chair. 'I suppose you think you can do a better job than Dad at dealing with me because you have religion.' She gave a mocking laugh. 'Well, don't bother, Blaze, because you and Dad are so alike it makes me sick. The only difference between you two is that you are arrogant enough to think you can have a positive impact on me.'

Blaze saw the spark of anger lighting Bonnie's eyes. He reached a subtle hand to hers. He felt the tension drain from her at his gentle, reassuring touch. He was used to his sister's hurtful comments. Bonnie would get used to them, too.

'I know I can't help you, but I'm hoping I can give you the time and space you need to heal.'

'Heal?' Beauty's eyes became dangerously dark. 'Heal from what? I'm not falling apart, so you can leave your counselling for those who need it. If that crazy driver hadn't swerved or whatever he was doing, his son would still be alive.'

'Beauty, that's callous and you know it.' His voice was calm and he could see the way Bonnie fought to control her mounting anger. It was always safer to say nothing when Beauty was in one of her moods.

Her dark eyes darted between the pair, giving them both a cold, hard look, then resting on Blaze. 'All I'm saying is that you and your precious, scarred girlfriend had better keep your distance. You can't get into my heart and mind, so you might as well leave me alone.'

Blaze shook his head in frustration, knowing the action would show Beauty she had achieved her goal, but was unable to help himself. 'You can throw your darts at me, Beauty, but leave Bonnie out of it. You and I are part of the reason Bonnie is scarred, remember? Now let's get a few things straight –'

'No! You need to get a few things straight, Blaze. I won't have you and Bonnie putting guilt on me about her burns. Bonnie decided to go in that burning stable, remember? I didn't force her.'

Blaze's anger was building, but Bonnie's calm voice stopped him. 'I've never blamed you, Beauty. In fact, I even thank God for that accident, because I would never have believed in him and got to know him if it hadn't happened.'

Beauty stared at Bonnie, speechless. Blaze took advantage of the silence.

'Now I have a few things you need to know,' His voice was confident again. 'You can only live here if you go to school, and you will live here under my rules. I want you to eat meals with Bonnie and me –'

'So I'm being used as a chaperone now?'

Blaze ignored her. 'And I expect you to let me know if you're going anywhere.'

'That's it?' Beauty asked after a few moments silence. 'No forcing me to go to church or attend your little youth counselling sessions?'

'That's up to you. You're welcome if you'd like to.'

Beauty jumped up from the table. 'No way! Since I'm not chained to you and the house, I might as well enjoy the freedom of choice I do have!'

She walked haughtily from the table, back to her room and slammed the door shut.

Bonnie couldn't suppress another smile. 'For someone so poised and beautiful, she sure has her moments.'

Blaze sighed. His sister's barbed comments had hurt a lot more than he had admitted. In truth, he knew there was no way he could help her. Only God could.

Chapter Six

Blaze answered the door. Bonnie had gone home to work on a uni assignment and Beauty was still shut in her room. He had been trying to prepare the youth Bible study all afternoon, but couldn't concentrate. If Beauty or Derek weren't on his mind, Bonnie was. Perhaps this visitor would be a welcome distraction.

'Danielle, come in!' He opened the door for the attractive teenager who stood there. There were rules about a pastor being alone with one of the youth he worked with, but Beauty was in her room, leaving Blaze with no qualms about asking Danielle in out of the cold.

Danielle stepped inside, wringing her hands and giving Blaze a shy, hesitant look. 'Blaze, I came over because I need to talk to you about some things.'

Blaze led her into the lounge room. 'To me?'

'Yeah. I know I'm supposed to talk to Bonnie, but I need to talk to a man; someone who understands how guys think.'

Blaze was cautious. 'Have a seat.' He rested his dark eyes on her, waiting for her to go on.

'Well, it's about Chappy. He and I have been going out for months, now. But he just doesn't seem serious. He's always clowning around.'

'And you want him to take a bit of time to listen and be himself?' Blaze guessed, thinking of the lively Chappy Eldwin. He certainly was amusing, but he could understand Danielle's frustration with him.

'That's not all.' Danielle avoided his eyes.

'What is it?'

At Blaze's gentle encouragement she looked up again. She took a deep breath.

'Well, I don't know if I really love him enough. I mean, I love him more than anyone else my age, but there's someone else I have more feelings for. The problem is, this other person is much older than me and he already has a girlfriend.'

Blaze stopped her. 'I think it would be good if you speak to Bonnie about this.'

She shook her head and looked about to cry. 'I know, I will. But first I need to know how a guy thinks.'

Blaze went to stop her, but she rushed on. 'So I need to know … say, if you and Bonnie loved each other, but weren't totally committed. How would you react if someone else came along and expressed their love for you? Would it ruin everything?'

Blaze couldn't suppress the surprise that passed over his face. He quickly masked it.'I don't know. I guess I'd have to be in that situation to know.'

Danielle sighed. 'It's just, well, I don't know if I should let him know how I feel before it's too late. I mean, what if he marries this girl but he doesn't really love her? What if I'm the one God really meant for him?'

Blaze saw her helpless desperation and wanted to laugh. The teenage romance dramas amongst the youth group were becoming more and more difficult to sort out. Her expression was now pleading.

'Please, Blaze? Can't you imagine for a minute how you'd feel if you were in that situation? You're a godly man. I want to know how you'd react.'

Blaze thought for a moment, wondering if he was treading on dangerous ground, but Danielle genuinely wanted to know. He knew she wouldn't be satisfied if he merely suggested she pray about it. It was avoiding the question.

'I guess if a guy wasn't committed to his girlfriend he'd be flattered.' His mind raced as he tried to take the attention away from how he, personally, would react. He had to make this example more general. 'He'd also be concerned about hurting your feelings if he didn't feel anything for you. I'd hope he was sensitive enough to be concerned, anyway.'

Danielle nodded, then looked up as Beauty came noisily into the room. Blaze watched in amazement as Danielle's expression changed in the instant she realised Beauty had been listening. Embarrassment and anger flashed across her face. 'And you are?' Her voice was cold, her face flushed.

Beauty smiled a tight smile. 'Living here. Like you wish you were. But don't mind me. Carry on pouring out your heart.'

'Beauty,' Blaze's tone was warning. Beauty gave an arrogant toss of her head, threw Danielle a sardonic smile and returned to her room. Blaze watched her go before turning back to the shocked Danielle.

'Sorry about that. Beauty is my little sister. She's come to stay for a while.'

Danielle's smile was forced. 'She's got a problem.'

What was he supposed to say to that? Yes, she did, but he wasn't going to divulge the intricacies of his sister's heart to Danielle.

'Guess I'd better go.' Danielle stood, looking uncomfortable. Blaze recognised that her confidence had been drained. There was no way she would be able to carry on the discussion now. But that was a good thing.

As Danielle left, Blaze had a strange feeling he had been rescued. He made his way back to his usual seat on the lounge. One by one, he screwed up pages of a newspaper and aimed them at the bin.

'Anyone home?'

Blaze jumped up in delight as Bonnie's cheerful voice rang through the screen door. He unlocked the door, gave her a hug and drew her into the lounge room. Before he could say a word, Beauty emerged from her room.

'You,' was all she said to Bonnie before settling herself by Blaze's side on the lounge and blocking Bonnie's way. Bonnie took another seat across the room.

'Yes, just me.' She threw Blaze a knowing grin before settling her gaze on Beauty. 'Who else?'

Beauty shrugged. 'I just wondered how many girls come around here. That Danielle is really pretty and interested in Blaze.'

'Beauty, that's enough!' Blaze's voice held an edge of steel. 'I wouldn't have even asked her in if you weren't home. Not that having you home helped in any way.'

'Why, Blaze,' Beauty said, in an apologetic tone which was definitely not genuine, 'Without me here, you couldn't have stopped her jumping into your lap.' She turned to Bonnie. 'Said she was here to talk about problems with her boyfriend, but she really just wanted to let Blaze know she was available.'

Bonnie stared at Beauty, then turned to Blaze, who was beginning to feel uncomfortable. 'I didn't see it like that.'

Bonnie looked to Beauty, then back to Blaze again. 'I thought Danielle and Chappy were pretty close.'

'It appears not,' Blaze admitted. 'Danielle has her heart set on someone else, but I didn't think it was my business to ask who he might be.'

Bonnie's eyes betrayed her hurt. 'I thought we agreed I would counsel the girls.'

Beauty patted Blaze's arm and gave a half smile. 'I'm sure you did, but Danielle knew her charms would work better on Blaze and Blaze thought he could help her more than you could.'

Blaze snatched his arm from beneath Beauty's hand. 'Go to your room, Beauty.' His voice was low and firm.

'So what am I? A child?'

'Go to your room!'

This time Beauty seemed to realise the depth of anger behind Blaze's calm facade. With a toss of her long, dark hair, she flounced from the room while Blaze turned back to Bonnie.

'I'm so sorry, Bonnie.' He reached a hand and she came to sit beside him. He let out a long, slow breath as his anger drained. His eyes were pleading with Bonnie to understand. 'I made a mistake. Danielle told me she needed a man's view on her relationship. I fell for it, but it won't happen again.'

Bonnie smiled and relief filled his heart. Trust Bonnie to be so understanding. Beauty might make his life difficult, but she'd never be able to come between them. One day he'd be able to convince Bonnie how much he loved her. One day she'd stop being so horribly aware of her scars and would be able to see herself the way he did; the way God did.

'It's okay, Blaze. I trust you.' She moved toward him, searching his eyes. Hope surged in his heart. She was initiating this. She wanted to kiss him enough that she had overcome her insecurities and initiated it. He smiled, warmth filling him. Her lips met with his and he drew her closer, his arms wrapping around her.

Chapter Seven

'That's Blaze's sister.' Danielle nudged Chappy as Beauty Clements walked in the school gate for her first day. Chappy looked up with interest, stopping his ridiculous ballet act for a moment. He saw past the hard expression on Beauty's face.

'She's terrified.'

Danielle let out a harsh laugh. 'Terrified? She's more like an eagle about to kill its prey.' She stopped short.

'What do you mean?' Chappy was suddenly interested. Clearly Danielle knew something more about Beauty.

'Never mind.' Danielle turned to lift her backpack from the ground and Chappy knew he wouldn't get anything else from her. He shrugged and resumed his ballet act, before theatrically running into a post and falling onto the ground in a heap.

He could see Danielle's attempt to ignore his antics but as usual she couldn't help laughing. She reached a hand to help him up from the ground. 'Come on, it's class time. Let's go.'

***

Beauty approached the principal's office, trying to ignore the sinking feeling she had inside. She had been too proud to admit to Blaze that morning that she was afraid. There was no way he could have imagined she was longing to run into his arms and be held like a child. She remembered the last time she had let him hold her. She had run to him for comfort after having a fight with Carrie, the daughter of the elephant trainer.

'Carrie said no one wants me,' Beauty had cried, knowing what her big brother's words would be.

'I want you.'

'Carrie said that when Mum died you said Storm and I should have died instead.'

Blaze had silently held her and she looked up into his face with complete trust. 'Blaze, I know you didn't say that. You should go and punch her out.'

A strange expression passed over Blaze's face and it was as though a knife slashed through her heart. In that moment she knew the truth. Of course Blaze would have wished she had died. He often spoke of their mother and how much he loved her and how hard it was without her. If Blaze had been given a choice …

She pulled back from his arms. 'Carrie's telling the truth, isn't she?'

When Blaze hesitated, she knew it was true.

'You hate me, too.' Her voice came out in a whispered sob.

'I don't hate you, Beauty. You're my little sister and I love you.'

Her eyes were wide and accusing. 'Then why did you say it?'

'Because I was so sad. And you cried a lot. I missed Mum so much and I needed her.'

'But Dad said everyone in the circus helped out.'

Blaze swallowed hard. 'Not at night they didn't. You needed feeding through the night and Dad needed me to help because there were two of you. I was so tired.'

His words gave no comfort to the grief stricken eight year old, who ran from him, refusing to come back when he called her name. From that day, she had become independent, striking out at anyone she could with her sharp wit.

Now she stood before the principal, still independent as ever.

The principal glanced over the form he held in his hand. 'This is your real name?'

His expression was friendly enough, but Beauty felt an instant dislike. She didn't blink and lied with practised ease. 'My real name's Amy. Beauty was my performing name when I was in the circus.'

'What do you prefer to be called?'

She shrugged. 'Amy will be fine.'

The principal nodded and crossed out the name on the form. Clearly, he preferred Amy to Beauty as well.

'I'll get someone to take you around the classrooms and have you signed on the roll.' He waved her out of his office dismissively, and seeing nothing else to do, Beauty went to sit in the seat outside to wait.

The principal kept his promise and it wasn't long before Beauty's guide appeared.

'Amy? I'm Dee. I've been asked to show you around.' The girl seemed shy and Beauty liked the feeling of power it gave her. With a hard smile, she picked up her school bag and followed Dee in silence.

The first classroom they entered was filled with students busily searching for note books in their school bags. Beauty noticed Danielle and the way she quickly averted her eyes. It was so much easier to make enemies than it was to make friends. She might as well stick with what she was good at. She held out the enrolment form for the teacher to sign, but the teacher was distracted.

'Where's Chappy?' She was glancing around the room and didn't notice Beauty's form until Beauty held it directly under her nose. Absently she took it, while a student called out from the back of the room.

'I think he had a dentist appointment.' Now Beauty took an interest. Something was going on. The student's voice had been too innocent and the rest of the class were watching closely.

'Again?' The teacher scribbled her signature onto the enrolment form. 'I thought he had one yesterday.'

The student nodded emphatically, as did many others in the room. The teacher shrugged and turned to a boy sitting by the doorway. 'Will you get the textbooks out, please Simon?'

Simon's nod was compliant as he headed to the back of the

room, then threw the other students a quick grin. The teacher still held Beauty's enrolment form but was distracted by Simon. He was standing at the text book cupboard, pulling and tugging at the door in a most convincing manner.

'It's stuck,' he called out. Still holding Beauty's form, the teacher headed to the back of the room. All fell deadly silent as she reached for the cupboard door and gave a mighty tug. She gave a squeal of fright as a figure jumped out of the cupboard with a yell. Beauty couldn't help laughing as the student rolled to the floor. The teacher gathered herself together and glared angrily at him.

'Chappy Eldwin, when will you ever grow up?'

Chappy chuckled as he picked himself up and headed to his seat.

Beauty was still laughing as Dee led her to the next classroom. It amazed her what laughter could do. Her heart felt lighter and she found herself smiling at Dee. 'That guy is crazy.'

Dee nodded and smiled back. 'Chappy Eldwin is the school clown. I've heard they call him Chappy after Charlie Chaplin, whoever that is.'

Beauty gave her a strange look. 'You've never heard of him? You know, the famous actor and comedian. About a hundred years ago. All the clowns in the circus idolise him.'

Dee nodded. 'Oh, that makes sense. Anyway, Chappy's always doing crazy things. I wish he was in more of our classes. We might not get much work done, but at least we'd have some fun.'

Beauty wished the same thing. If Chappy Eldwin were anything like the real Charlie Chaplin he might be worth getting to know.

Dee was looking at her with interest. 'I heard you were from a circus.'

'Yeah, but we left years ago.'

'Do you still ride horses?'

Beauty shook her head, wondering how Dee knew about her past but refusing to think about Montford Express. She would never ride a horse again. Beauty had ridden horses. This new Amy Clements would not.

'I've always wanted a horse,' Dee said, 'but we live too far from any decent blocks of land to keep one. I remember trying to convince Dad to let me keep one in my room when I was younger.'

She laughed at the memory and Beauty smiled, deciding Dee wasn't so bad. As long as she minded her own business they might get along okay.

***

Blaze invited Beauty to join in the Bible study in the lounge room that night, but she insisted on staying in her room. Her pride was stronger than her curiosity and she gave Blaze a cold look. 'I don't need or want your religion. I've got better things to do.'

Blaze appeared nonplussed. 'You're welcome to come out for supper and just get to know people.'

Beauty was about to tell him she didn't need religious friends and it irritated her that he left before she had the chance.

She lay on her bed, staring at the picture of Montford Express on her wall. It was pure stubbornness that stopped her letting Blaze fix it for her. It was one of Blaze's best paintings and was so lifelike it could be mistaken for a photo. If only he had got the white on the legs right.

The cheerful sound of young people arriving teased her and she put a pillow over her head to block it out. Then she heard Chappy Eldwin's voice and curiosity got the better of her. She moved to the door and listened to the playful banter going on. Then it became quiet and Blaze's deep voice could be heard. She pressed her ear against the door to listen.

'When the doctor said I had tetanus and might not make it I began to think more seriously about what I had spent my time in life doing …'

Beauty moved away and buried her head in a book. She didn't want to think about the time Blaze had nearly died. She hated all the regrets and questions about life and death that had plagued her. It was too overwhelming. She tried to shut them out, just as she had done ever since but they wouldn't go away. She stared at the picture of Montford Express on her wall and remembered Blaze's horse, Peter Pan. He had been the first to succumb to tetanus, but Blaze had been next. And it was all her fault. Her mind went back to the week before he collapsed. They had been out riding and she had loved the freedom of being out in the fresh air, cantering along with her siblings the way they had in their circus days. But then Blaze had called it short, reminding them they needed to get back and do their school homework.

She had ignored him, but Storm grabbed at her leg to stop her riding past. 'Come on, Beauty, you heard the boss-man. We have to go.' She shook herself free, knowing Storm was just as annoyed about having to go as she was. But then Blaze whistled to Montford Express and to her annoyance, her horse obediently went to him. She tried to ride away, but Montford refused to leave Blaze. The fact that her horse was showing more loyalty to Blaze than her, made her see red. She leaped from his back and charged at the surprised Blaze, knocking him back onto the barbed wire fence. Blaze's expression was hurt and she didn't miss the way he looked down at his arm. A small cut was seeping blood.

'Beauty, I don't want to go either.' His voice was quiet, sad. 'But school is the whole reason Dad made us leave the circus.'

'No, Blaze, you and your stupid God are the reason we left! No one in the circus can stand your religion, and neither can I!'

With that she had stormed off to the house. No one had mentioned the barbed wire cut on his arm, but it got infected by tetanus and almost cost him his life. It was her fault. Blaze had never mentioned it to her, and she wondered if he even remembered how he got the cut. He had been delirious for days.

She let out a weary sigh. Blaze might not know it was her fault, but she did. It was as though she was cursed. Whatever she did was sure to hurt someone and there was nothing she could do about it. She had stopped trying to be nice; had stopped letting herself care a long time ago. But every now and then the memories would sneak up on her and she would let herself care before she even realised.

Beauty knew when the talk was over. The muffled voices became louder and she could hear the voices spread as the group moved throughout the house. She quietly opened her bedroom door and stood in the doorway, watching. No one seemed to notice her. Blaze was talking to some of the youth and others seemed deep in thought. She felt defensive – surely some of them must have guessed Blaze's near-fatal illness was her fault? Sometimes she felt as though the world was looking at her, pointing, accusing. Her eyes were drawn to Chappy who was more lighthearted than any of the others. He collected a biscuit then rushed to the lounge, causing the girls to jump up with a squeal as he dived into the middle of the seat.

Blaze looked up, distracted from his conversation. 'Chappy ...' His tone was half warning, half amused.

'What's up?' Chappy grinned as he settled himself into the seat and looked at the girls now across the other side of the room. 'Scared of boy germs?'

Danielle glared at him. 'Scared of being impounded into the seat, more like it!'

'Impounded?' Chappy chuckled, not put off by her fierce glare. 'Where did you manage to pick up a word like that?'

Danielle screwed up her nose in mock disgust. 'If you ever managed to listen in class instead of being a distraction you might just know what it means.'

Chappy sat up straighter, his eyes challenging. 'So what does it mean?'

'Can't you work it out from the context?'

'Yes, I know what you think it means, but I want to know if you really know what it means.'

Danielle shrugged and moved to another seat while the other girls settled back onto the lounge beside Chappy, but he didn't let it go. He looked up and his eyes caught Beauty still standing by her door.

'Hey, Beauty!'

Beauty ignored him. He knew she had been introduced as Amy by the school and she refused to respond. She saw Blaze glance to her, his expression concerned. What was his problem? Did he think she would attack Chappy?

'Amy!' Chappy tried again. This time she looked at him.

He grinned in satisfaction. 'Got a dictionary?'

Beauty nodded.

'Can you look up "impounded" please? For Danielle's benefit.'

Beauty held in her smile. Chappy's expression was so mischievous, but she couldn't let him see it affected her. She ducked into her room and collected the pocket dictionary from her school bag. Frowning, she ran her eyes down the words, then headed out to the lounge room.

'It's a real word.' Danielle was clearly trying to sound convinced. 'I know it's there.'

'It is.' Beauty ran her finger down the page and stopped at the word. 'It means to confiscate or take legal possession of, like putting an animal in the pound.'

Chappy laughed victoriously. 'Would you believe Danielle reckoned I just threatened to take legal possession of her? Does that mean I threatened to marry her?'

Beauty felt herself blushing for no apparent reason.

'Come on Beauty. I need your support here.'

Beauty saw the way Blaze took a step forward, ready to intervene if necessary. But before he could, Chappy came and took her hand, leading her into the middle of the group. 'What does a man taking legal possession of a woman mean to you?'

Beauty tried to pull back, but he held her hand tightly as he urged her to answer the question.

'Come on, Beauty …'

Beauty. He was calling her that again and she'd forgotten to correct him. No doubt if she looked up at him there would be a triumphant grin on his face. He let go of her hand and casually slung his arm over her shoulder. She flung it off. 'I don't know. Ask Danielle.'

Chappy went to reach for her again, but she saw the way Blaze subtly shook his head. Chappy took the hint and let her go.

Beauty escaped to her room while she could, shutting the door behind her. She could hear laughing and talking and above it all, Chappy Eldwin's cheerful voice. She liked him, much to her own annoyance. She looked down at her hand. Who else in her life dared take her hand or put an arm around her shoulder? What was wrong with the guy? Couldn't he see how unapproachable and unlovable she was? She'd have to work harder to show him.

Chapter Eight

Bonnie was surprised to hear the youth from school calling Beauty 'Amy'. As they left she came to Beauty's door and knocked. When she received no answer she tentatively opened the door. Beauty was on her bed, looking at something in her hand.

'I just had a question.'

Beauty grunted. 'Yeah?'

'I heard them calling you Amy.'

Beauty didn't look up. 'It was my mother's name.'

'What's wrong with your name?'

Beauty looked up and Bonnie tried to catch a glimpse of what she was holding. It looked like a crumpled piece of paper with some kind of sketch on it.

Beauty swallowed hard and if Bonnie hadn't known better she would have thought Beauty was holding back tears. But then her eyes began flashing their usual sparks. 'You have no idea what it's like to have everyone judge you, to compare you with your name and see if you live up to it.' Beauty glared at Bonnie. 'Starre should have been called Beauty, not me!'

Bonnie listened in surprise. Did it bother Beauty that her sister was more breathtakingly beautiful? What other hurts lay beneath Beauty's tough exterior?

'I don't think anyone thinks that way,' Bonnie assured her, but fell silent as Beauty shook her head vigorously.

'How can you say that? Remember how you were teased about

your scars after your accident? Don't you remember what it was like to have everyone judge you?'

Bonnie tried not to show how shocked she was. Did Beauty actually care? She remembered back to the day the Clements family had first visited her in hospital and the look on Beauty's face. It had been filled with anguish and guilt. Surely Beauty didn't still blame herself for asking Bonnie to go into the burning stables? Apart from that very first day, Beauty had been cold and insensitive whenever the fire was mentioned.

'I remember.' Bonnie's voice was gentle as she ran her finger along one of the scars down her arm. 'But I've been able to heal and I rarely consider what other people are thinking of my scars anymore.' Even as Bonnie spoke the words, she knew they were not entirely true. Deep within was a fear that someday Blaze may find her scars repulsive.

Beauty sat up, throwing her legs over the side of the bed. 'How can you act as though the accident never happened? How can you live as though it doesn't matter how you look? You nearly died, Bonnie! You used to be so popular, so pretty.'

Beauty stopped and Bonnie wondered if she had just realised the implication of her words. Poor Beauty. She was so lost. There was so much she could say, but what would reach Beauty Clements? She had to choose her words carefully.

'There's a lot more to true beauty than meets the eye. What I learned through the accident is that it's what's in your heart that really matters.'

Beauty was clearly not buying it. She screwed up her pretty face. 'According to who? If it really was the heart, I wouldn't have so many people staring at me all the time.'

Suddenly Bonnie understood. 'I reckon those people only stare at you because they're fascinated by you. A circus girl who is a twin and has siblings who are triplets is a bit unusual, don't you think?'

Beauty's pained expression softened for a moment. Encouraged, Bonnie made the mistake of continuing. 'You are beautiful, Beauty, and people enjoy looking at you. I believe they want to get to know you; have you for a friend.'

Beauty shook her head in disgust. 'I don't need your flattery, Bonnie.'

Bonnie knew she had just wiped out the value of her other words as well. If only she hadn't spoken of outward beauty. Why did it matter so much to people – including herself? Why couldn't Beauty see herself the way other people did?

The thought jarred her. Wasn't she exactly the same? Her mother kept telling her how attractive she was, burns and all, but she couldn't accept it. So did she truly believe her own words?

Slowly, she began to smile. 'Yes, Lord, I do believe it.' It was time she lived out her belief and stopped doubting Blaze's love for her. And more importantly, it was time she stopped doubting God's love for her. God had made her whole and complete on the inside, and that overflowed. Scars or no scars, she was beautiful because God made her beautiful.

***

Beauty hadn't believed Bonnie at the time but she decided to test her theory and see if people might like to be her friend. So when a year twelve student bumped roughly past her on his way to class she made an effort not to chase after him and shove him back. She even accepted the apology he threw over his shoulder.

'No worries.' She managed a smile and felt proud of herself.

He stopped and turned back. 'Hey, aren't you the new girl from the circus?'

He appeared interested, not mocking.

'Yes. I left the circus a while ago, though.'

He came and stood before her, his expression friendly. 'Want to join me and my mates for a game of tennis at lunch?'

Beauty nodded and he smiled. It seemed she was doing a good job of being the pleasant Amy Clements. And she had to admit it was nice to have this good looking year twelve boy smiling at her rather than making snide comments behind her back.

Beauty had never played tennis before, but she found herself looking forward to lunch time rather than dreading it as she had in her last school. She assumed she would pick the game up quickly as she did most sports.

'I'm Nate Owen,' the year twelve boy introduced himself as she arrived at the tennis courts. He looked around at his friends. 'This is the new girl. I invited her to have a game with us.'

The group looked at her with curiosity and she remind herself it was probably friendly. She gave them a tight smile. 'I'm Amy.'

Nate handed her a racquet. 'Well, why don't you and I have a hit first? See what you're capable of?'

There was something patronising in his tone and Beauty frowned before she could stop herself. 'And how about I see what you're capable of?'

He raised his brows at the bite in her tone and chuckled. 'Let's just do that.'

Beauty bit her lip. She would have to try harder to be nice. She always seemed to rile people up. But they riled her up first.

Nate stood poised, racquet in one hand, ball in the other. He gave her a smug look, then swung the racquet hard. Beauty did her best to hit the ball, but Nate was clearly well practiced at tennis and knew exactly where to place it. She grunted in frustration as the ball sailed past her racquet.

Nate grinned at her. 'Who's showing who, circus girl?'

Nate's group of friends laughed but Beauty managed to bite her tongue and focus on the ball. Nate poised his racquet again. She lunged at the ball but missed again.

Nate lifted his hands in question. 'Are you blind or something?

'The sun is in my eyes.' It was an excuse, but she could feel familiar warmth filling her, starting somewhere deep inside and beginning to build.

Be nice, she told herself, gritting her teeth as the ball was served once again. She knew Nate was deliberately serving the ball with great speed and skill and then laughing at her as she missed it.

'Can't you give me a fair go?'

Nate paused, racquet high in the air. 'What do you mean?'

He knew exactly what she meant and Beauty hated the way all his year twelve friends laughed. 'Can't you hit it toward me, rather than where only a professional could get it?'

Nate shrugged. It seemed he was enjoying this chance to ruffle the new girl. 'Okay.'

Beauty stood poised and waited for the serve, determined not to miss. Nate hit the ball with force, this time directly at Beauty. She flung herself aside as the ball whizzed past.

Feeling uncontrollable anger welling up within, Beauty set it free. 'That could have killed me!' she screamed, flinging down her racquet. She charged toward the net, hands on hips.

Nate grinned. 'Not if you had hit it. Which is what you're supposed to do.'

His friends all laughed again and Beauty lost it. Flipping her body backward over the net and cartwheeling until she stood eye to eye with Nate, she glared into his face. His jaw dropped as he stared at her. He began to smile, but it died on his face as she flung the tennis ball hard into his chest. She picked up another as he rubbed his chest, and this time she flung it into his face.

'Hey, cut it out,' one of his female friends called as Nate's lip began to bleed.

'Make me!' Beauty responded angrily, holding another tennis ball poised. Nate's friend lunged at her and she flung herself aside.

'Fight, fight!' a boy began chanting. Others joined in and Beauty turned to face the girl who had defended Nate. A swearing match began between the two and a crowd quickly gathered.

It wasn't long before a teacher arrived, pushing his way through the crowd.

'What's going on?' He stepped between the red faced Beauty and Nate's friend who couldn't seem to stop the string of insults coming from her mouth.

'This new girl threw tennis balls at Nate. Look at his lip.'

Beauty was infuriated. 'He tried to hit me with it first!' This wasn't her fault and she wasn't going to let anyone think it was. She looked up to see Danielle watching. A satisfied smile covered her pretty face and Beauty wished she could strike it from her.

'I told you,' Danielle whispered to Chappy, while Chappy tried to silence her. Beauty came toward them, her eyes dark. 'You told him what, Danielle?'

The teacher interrupted. 'All three of you come with me.' He pointed to Nate, his female friend and Beauty. Glaring back at the crowd, Beauty shook her head. They all stood on the tennis court, watching her in stunned silence. No doubt they were wondering what had happened to the pleasant Amy Clements.

'I give up,' Beauty thought to herself as she spent the afternoon standing against the brick wall outside the principal's office. 'I might as well be myself again.'

***

Beauty handed Bonnie a note, glad Blaze wasn't there when she arrived home from school.

'Bonnie, will you sign this for me? I don't want Blaze to see it.'

Bonnie took the piece of paper. Beauty waited while she read over the details of the fight that had occurred that day. She looked up and studied Beauty's defiant expression. 'What happened?'

'They deserved it.'

'What did they do?'

'Wouldn't give me a fair go at tennis.'

'So you threw a tennis ball at Nate Owen?'

Beauty crossed her arms. 'He tried to get me first. He's one of those guys who thinks he's so good. I can't stand him!'

Bonnie shook her head. Beauty had known she wouldn't sign the form on Blaze's behalf, but it had been worth a try. There was no way she was going to show Blaze. She would just have to do detention. Despite denying it to everyone else she knew deep down that she deserved it. If she had kept her cool like she had planned she wouldn't be in this position.

'Beauty, what makes you hate everyone so much?'

Beauty screwed her nose up at Bonnie. 'I don't hate everyone.'

'Well, what makes you feel you have to dislike and hurt everyone?'

Beauty had no answer for a long time. When she looked up, she sighed. How could she tell Bonnie the truth; that she was doomed to a lifetime of hurting anyone who crossed her path and that it was impossible to love anyone when she hated herself? She took the form back from Bonnie's hand. 'Don't worry about the note.'

Beauty felt vulnerable and she hated the feeling. Why did Bonnie's caring ways have that effect on her? Was it because she knew Bonnie prayed for her and there was nothing she could do about it? Or was it because, deep down, she knew it was her fault Bonnie had nearly died in the fire all those years ago? If anything, Bonnie should hate her. It would be easier if she did.

Beauty's failure to show Blaze her form landed her on detention for a week. She thought she wouldn't mind sitting outside the principal's office each lunchtime if it meant she could have a break from trying to make friends and be nice. However, Nate Owen had also failed to show his parents the form. He smirked as the principal directed them to the seats outside his office.

'Can you two sit there in a civilised manner without talking?'

Beauty would have liked to say no, but Nate nodded. 'Yes, sir. We can.' He gave Beauty a sideways grin. Not knowing how to respond, Beauty stared at her feet. She intended to stay looking at her feet all lunchtime, but was distracted when she heard Nate rustling in his school bag. She watched as he took out some correction fluid and began writing something on the sole of his shoe. The school receptionist looked up from her desk a few metres away and Nate immediately stopped and hid the forbidden fluid. He gave the receptionist a friendly nod, then continued work once she looked away. Finally he put the correction fluid away, then changed his seating position. Beauty couldn't help looking at the sole of his shoe which was now clearly displayed.

'Sorry!' was written clearly in white across the black sole. Stunned, Beauty glanced at him and then away again. It didn't look like he was making fun of her. In fact, his look was friendly. She couldn't remember anyone apologising to her before, especially when she was as much to blame for the problem.

It was the first of Nate's attempts to reach her and Beauty found herself looking forward to their lunch time detentions. Every day, Nate would have a new message written on the sole of his shoe for her to read. Yet as soon as lunch ended, he would jump up from the seat and disappear before she had a chance to say anything. The messages ranged from anything as simple as 'hello', to some things as corny as 'bare your sole.' They always brought a smile to her face and she was disappointed when their final day of detention came.

The principal called them in for a last warning. 'You two had better be mature enough to be let loose in the school grounds again at lunchtime.'

'We are.' Nate grinned. 'I think this time of detention has given Amy a chance to get to know me a bit more. I don't think she'll attack me next time I joke around with her.'

The principal frowned. 'The rules were no talking.'

Nate nodded. 'I know. We didn't talk. Ask the office ladies.'

The principal ignored him. 'Alright you two, out of here. And I don't want to see either of you here again!'

Beauty expected Nate to rush off, but he waited for her to collect her bag, then walked by her side from the office. He shoved his hands in his pockets.

'I wanted to ask you something, Amy.' He stopped and she waited, curious. 'I wondered if you will go out with me. You know, come to parties with me and stuff. I know we didn't get off to a good start, but I think you could be a lot of fun if you had someone to help you relax a bit.'

Beauty wondered what he meant. She presumed he was talking

about the year twelve parties she had often heard about. The ones where those who were old enough bought alcohol for the others to share. She smiled up at Nate. Perhaps a good party was what she needed. And Blaze hadn't specifically told her 'no alcohol'. What he didn't know wouldn't hurt him.

'Will you?' Nate pressed and she nodded, wondering if her response was enthusiastic enough. Nate obviously thought so as he gave her a satisfied grin then reached for her hand. 'I knew you weren't as irrational as you pretended to be.'

She snatched her hand back and he held up his hands in mock surrender. 'Just joking.'

There was a sparkle in his eyes and the anger drained from her as she laughed. Nate might just be good for her.

Chapter Nine

The weather was warming up and Blaze organised a barbecue at the local pool for anyone who cared to come. He invited Beauty and she studied him suspiciously.

'Why would I come?'

'Because it will be fun.'

'So no preaching? No deep, soppy talks or anything?'

Blaze laughed. 'No. I was actually thinking of Derek when I arranged this. I'm hoping he will come and make some friends and I don't think he would appreciate preaching.'

Beauty shrugged. 'Derek? That teenager you found drunk? Fine, I'll come.' She chuckled at Blaze's surprised look. 'What? You asked me. And I like having a bit of fun, too.'

'I know. And I have to admit you've been a lot more relaxed and happy lately.'

'Yeah, having a boyfriend is good for me.'

Blaze stopped in his tracks. 'You have a boyfriend?'

Beauty didn't answer, but a challenge was in her eyes.

Blaze didn't blink. 'You going to invite him to the barbecue so I can meet him?'

Beauty screwed up her nose. 'No. Somehow I don't think an alcohol-free pool party is Nate's kind of thing.'

Blaze's eyebrows shot up. 'Now that bothers me. What kind of a person is this boyfriend of yours?'

'Don't go getting all protective. He's my choice and there's nothing you can do about it.'

Blaze disagreed. 'I can, little sister. I can pray for your protection, and I do. Every day.'

Beauty rolled her eyes. 'I'd tell you not to bother but I know it won't stop you.'

'You're right. It won't.'

Beauty wanted to smile but stopped herself. She was showing enough vulnerability by going to the pool in the first place. She didn't want anyone to think she was actually happy about it. Yet she found herself looking forward to the event and wondering what Derek would be like. If he was a drunk with hardly any friends he probably had issues, and she of all people understood what it was like to have issues.

The moment she arrived at the pool she searched for him discreetly. Most of the youth group were there, along with a few of their friends from school. Derek must be the lanky, dark haired stranger sitting in the middle of a group of girls but not looking very happy about it. He looked uncomfortable and bored and one by one the girls moved away. She saw Blaze leave his post at the barbeque to talk to him. Derek nodded at something Blaze said, then took out a cigarette. Blaze directed him to the smoking area, then went back to join Bonnie at the barbeque. Derek stood by himself looking sullen and unapproachable. Beauty wondered why Blaze even bothered with Derek. Clearly it was impossible to change who you were deep down inside.

Feeling awkward, she glanced around. Blaze and Bonnie were busy cooking at the barbecue and she didn't have the courage to approach anyone else. Maybe she could go to the kiosk and buy an ice cream. Then at least she wouldn't be just standing on her own, looking lost.

Resolute, she headed toward the kiosk. As she neared, she noticed the cheerful Chappy Eldwin heading that way from the other direction. He was amongst a group of girls from school and for once Danielle wasn't one of them.

They had just about reached the kiosk when the girls with Chappy broke into a run and arrived noisily at the shop window. The group were just ahead of Beauty and she stepped back, eyeing them warily.

'Hey, you pushed in!' Chappy complained to the girls.

They rounded on him. 'On who?'

'On my young friend here.' Chappy put an arm around Beauty's shoulder as though they were best friends. She shrugged away.

The girls looked truly apologetic. 'Sorry Amy.'

'Sorry, we didn't realise.'

The girls were stepping back away from the window, but Beauty shook her head. 'Ignore Chappy. He couldn't care less about me. He's just trying to get himself to the front of the line. You're not the ones who should be apologising for bad manners.'

'Hey, you traitor!' Chappy's face became an expression of mock betrayal and Beauty wanted to laugh but held it in.

She pointed the girls back to the front of the line. 'Stay there. You were here first.'

Chappy tried to move around the girls, but they blocked his way and insisted Beauty go to the front of the line. It defeated her purpose of filling in time, but the further she was from Chappy, the better.

She was heading toward the bin with her ice cream wrapper when Chappy left his coveted place in line and headed her way. She watched him warily.

'I think you're the one who needs to learn some manners, young Miss Clements.' There was a playful gleam in his eyes as he approached.

'Don't come near me,' Beauty warned, a hint of panic in her voice.

Chappy smiled his spontaneous smile and shook his head. 'I don't think you have a right to tell anyone what they can or can't do after that cheeky performance back there.' He came a step closer. Beauty saw he would not back off and she didn't really want to hurt him, so she decided to make her escape. She turned and fled, with Chappy close behind. She charged toward Blaze who still stood at the barbeque turning sausages.

'Blaze! Stop him!'

Blaze looked up but didn't have time to react. Chappy Eldwin had Beauty in his firm hold and was dragging her toward the pool, still fully clothed.

'Chappy, I don't think that's a good idea.' Blaze stopped as the inevitable splash came.

Beauty came up spluttering and the first thing she saw was Blaze, frozen in place at the barbeque, apprehension showing clearly in his eyes. She shook her head and struggled to the water's edge, searching for Chappy. Where was he? He was in serious trouble now. Her eyes caught him just as he escaped into the men's showers. It was then that she noticed what was in her hand. A bare paddle-pop stick, the remnant of her ice cream. Oh well, she hadn't wanted it anyway. She'd only bought it to give herself something to do. And it had worked.

'Food's ready,' Blaze called, so she headed to the barbecue area, still trying to catch her breath. Blaze shook his head at her in disbelief. 'I never know what to expect from you, little sister.'

Beauty shrugged. 'I'll get him later. I can't really go into the men's showers, can I?'

Blaze just looked at her and she searched herself for an explanation for why she wasn't really upset. *It's something to do with Chappy*, she told herself. She could get revenge on him but what good would it do? She didn't want to hurt him, not really.

Beauty collected some food and sat to the side of the noisy teenagers. Hugging her arms across her chest, she wished she had brought a towel. She hadn't intended to swim and so didn't come prepared.

'Can we sit here?'

Beauty nodded at the group of girls who took their place beside her. Despite being so cold and wet, a warmth filled her somewhere deep inside. At least these girls were making an effort. She didn't want to be like Derek who still stood alone, refusing to be brought into the group and looking subdued and unhappy.

'I think I at least owe you this.'

Beauty looked up into Chappy's face as he placed his towel around her shivering shoulders. She began to push it off, but stopped when she saw the expression on Danielle's face. It was something between scorn and hatred. Well, she would accept the towel just to spite her. If Danielle thought there was something going on between her and Chappy, she might as well give her the full performance.

She stood, threw down the towel and faced Chappy with a grin. 'I think I owe you this.'

Her hand came out and she wiped the piece of bread she held down his cheek, leaving a smear of butter. His brows shot up and a chuckle escaped him.

'You ... you little horror!'

'No, this would make me a horror.' She grabbed the bottle of tomato sauce from a nearby table and squirted him fair in the face. He gasped and stared at her, but his eyes sparkled with amusement.

'Now that was going one step too far!' He took a step forward but she grabbed his arm.

'I think you need a wash off, Chappy. You're a bit of a mess.' She began dragging him toward the pool, surprised and wary when he didn't struggle. It wasn't until they stood right at the water's edge that he looked straight at her, his mischievous grin widening and a clear challenge in his eyes.

'What now, Miss Clements?'

'You go in, that's what.'

'You think so?'

Beauty didn't hesitate as she gave him a mighty shove. At the same time, he grabbed her around the waist, pulling her in with him. When she came up this time, he was centimetres from her face, his eyes level with hers. He was laughing as he shook the water from his hair and into her eyes.

He gave her a challenging look as he grabbed her arms to stop her getting away. 'Are we even yet?'

Beauty pretended to consider and he quirked an eyebrow at her. 'If we're not, I'll have to put you under again.'

He was grinning, but she knew he would do it. She gave him a small, brief smile. 'Okay, I think it's safe to say we're even.'

'One last thing.' His smile was gone.

'What's that?'

'I need you to smile again.'

'What?'

'Smile or I'll have to put you under. It's the rules.'

He was just so ridiculous that she found her smile came easily. And it was then she realised his hands were now around her waist. She should shove him away; show him he couldn't touch her and get away with it. But she had to admit she didn't want to shove him away.

She was distracted from her confusing thoughts when Chappy looked up to the edge of the pool. 'We have an audience,' he told her quietly.

She glanced up to see he was right. Everyone was watching them. She took a deep breath. 'Sorry, but I have to keep my reputation.'

With that, she shoved him away from her with a force that pushed him backward and under the water again. Then she swam full speed to the edge of the pool, glared at the onlookers and ran into the girl's showers without looking back. She sat shivering in one of the shower cubicles, completely confused. Way too many feelings were demanding her attention and she couldn't seem to ignore or push them away like she used to.

***

Beauty still sat alone in a shower cubicle when Danielle's voice floated into the building.

'Chappy is always challenged by the difficult cases but I think Blaze's sister is a lost cause. If Blaze can't reach her, who can?'

'I know,' another voice agreed. 'Chappy's just too nice for his own good sometimes.'

'Did you see her attack Nate Owen?'

'No, but I can imagine those pretty little claws could do some damage!'

Was that why Chappy made an effort to be nice; to put his arm around her? Beauty felt pain squeeze around her heart and knew she had made a mistake. She had promised herself a long time ago that she wouldn't let anyone close enough to hurt her again. So why had let those barriers down? If Christians really saw her as a challenge, a project to work on, she wanted nothing more to do with them or their meetings.

Chapter Ten

Blaze was adjusting his tie when the phone rang.

'Can you come over, mate?' Derek's familiar voice asked. He had already called twice that day and a few times every day since the barbecue.

Blaze glanced at Bonnie, all dressed up for their night out together. 'What's up, Derek?'

'I just wanted someone to talk to, mate. It's pretty quiet over here.'

'I'm about to go out with Bonnie.'

'That girl of yours? Well, it's just I didn't want to be tempted to go to the pub or anything. You know how it is when you're all alone.'

Blaze withheld a sigh. He knew Derek's manipulative ways and this was going to be a special night. 'Sorry, Derek. Not tonight. Haven't you got someone else you could spend time with?'

'No one. I'm completely alone.'

'Well what about if I bring a DVD over for you to watch?'

Derek's voice became angry. 'Don't worry about it, mate. I want real friends, not charity. I'll do my own thing.'

He hung up and Blaze turned to Bonnie to explain. 'Derek wanting some company. I told him I'm not available tonight and he got a bit upset.' He shrugged then took her hand. 'Let's go.' He offered a quick prayer for Derek, then put him out of his mind.

Once they sat quietly in the restaurant, Blaze studied Bonnie's bright blue eyes. Tenderness warmed him at her tentative smile. He had no doubts about what he was about to do. Bonnie was the one for him. She always had been. 'Bonnie, there's some things I need to talk to you about.'

Her brows lifted as she waited patiently. He knew he had her full attention and he loved that about her. If he had something to say she would listen as though every word were important, as though committing it to heart and memory.

'I've been thinking a lot about Sky lately.' He spoke of his brother's child. Sky had been born three years ago to Blaze's brother, Prince. Prince had still been a child of sixteen at the time and refused to accept any responsibility for her. When Sky's teenager mother also abandoned her, Blaze took on the role of guardian. However, having grown up without a mother and father figure himself, he insisted she be fostered out to a Christian couple for the time being.

'What have you been thinking?' Bonnie pressed. 'Is she okay?'

'She's fine,' Blaze assured her, though there was a wistful tone to his voice. 'I just can't help thinking about her all the time. And I worry about her. I think she needs her real family.'

Bonnie nodded. 'She does.'

Blaze pictured his niece with her long, dark, hair and olive complexion. She looked so like his sisters it was uncanny. He had always taken the guardianship of his brothers and sisters seriously and it was the same for Sky.

Bonnie put a hand on his, capturing his attention again. 'Do you think you should bring her here?'

Blaze sighed. 'I don't know. I'm hardly ever home, really. What would she do while I work?'

'Is that the only problem?'

Blaze shook his head, marvelling at the way Bonnie seemed to read his mind. 'No,' he admitted. 'I also want her to have a mother. I grew up with only a father, and I don't want her to go through the same thing.'

'You need to get yourself a wife!' Bonnie teased, and a slow smile began at the corners of Blaze's mouth.

'You know, I had been thinking the same kind of thing.'

Suddenly nervous, he stood. The restaurant was becoming crowded. True, they hadn't eaten yet, but he needed to get out of here. He reached a hand to the surprised Bonnie. 'Let's go.'

She didn't question him, but he saw the concern in her eyes. He merely smiled. He knew he was making the right decision. He was not going to let this night be ordinary. Especially now he knew she shared his concern for little Sky and would want to do what was best for her.

***

Bonnie wondered what was going on with Blaze. He was different tonight. Confident as usual, but restless. As they walked around the park in the late evening air, she chatted about her day, trying to put him at ease. When she fell silent for a few moments, Blaze drew her close to his side.

'I spoke to your father yesterday, Bonnie.'

Bonnie's heart beat faster at his tone. Did that mean what she thought it meant? She needed to keep light-hearted until she knew for sure.

Giving him a cheeky look, she grinned up into his face. 'You often speak to my father.'

Blaze chuckled and tightened his hold. 'Not like I did yesterday. Bonnie, I love you so much. Sometimes I don't know how to express it, but I know you're amazing. The way you reach those young people. The way you've come through so much. I've never met anyone like you.'

Bonnie smiled and ran her fingers gently down his cheek. 'I think you're pretty special too.'

He caught her hand and reached into his pocket. 'I have something to ask you.'

Her heart began to pound hard in her chest. She knew what was coming. He was so confident and full of purpose.

He held one of her hands while holding something out to her and gazing deep into her eyes. 'Will you marry me, Bonnie Blake?'

Bonnie nodded, not even bothering to look at the ring. It was Blaze she was interested in; Blaze she had always loved. She found for the first time she could look into those dark, intense eyes without feeling the need to turn away. Blaze Clements loved her enough to

62

marry her!

***

Beauty pretended she couldn't care less when Blaze and Bonnie announced their engagement to her that evening, but she felt sick inside. Something about their happiness scared her and reminded her how unhappy her own heart was. She fiddled with a paper clip she had found on the floor. 'So when's the wedding?'

'We thought six months would be best.' Blaze was unable to keep the depth of his feelings from showing every time he looked at his fiancée.

'And what about me?' Beauty's hands went to her hips. 'Do I get put out on the street?'

Blaze laughed, ruffling his sister's hair and earning himself a glare. 'Of course not. You're still part of the family. And Sky will be, too.'

'Sky?' Beauty was surprised. 'Is that what this is all about? Getting yourself a mother for Sky and me? I don't need a mother!'

Bonnie chuckled at Beauty's ferocity. 'As if I could be a mother to you, Beauty. I'm only a few years older. I wouldn't mind being a sister, though. I've never had a sister.'

'Well I have plenty,' Beauty's eyes now flashed sparks, 'and I certainly don't need another one.'

Beauty saw the hurt flash across Bonnie's face and hated herself for ruining the moment. Why did she do it? It was like something rose up from deep within her and broke free, destroying the happiness of anyone around her.

***

Derek Sheen sat alone in his bedroom, his anger mounting. He had thought of suicide many times before. The time his mother confessed she had never really loved his father. The time she had admitted she only sought custody of him for the money she would get from the government. There were the many times life seemed just too hard, too empty and hopeless. He had known that suicide would just be giving up. No one would miss him and he would not be able to make sure people knew he existed.

However, tonight was different. The compassionate youth pastor from the church would care if he commited suicide and that gave Derek a sense of power. He wanted to make someone hurt the way he had hurt all his life. He wanted to make someone feel guilty, the way he felt guilty just for being alive and being a burden on other people. Tonight would be the night when Derek took control. He would finally be significant.

Derek searched through his school bag for a pen and piece of paper and in scrawled hand, began to write. The more he wrote, the more the resentment of years of rejection built up within him. Soon this would be the handsome, compassionate Blaze Clements' problem. The burden would be gone.

'I'm sorry, Blaze,' he wrote, 'but I just couldn't cope tonight. I thought you would care enough to come and see me, but obviously there are times when you are selfish and unable to hear what other people are saying. I thought you understood my pain. I thought you listened and I started to believe in God. But after tonight, I don't. I prayed that if God was real, you would come and talk to me and tell me about him so I could become a Christian. But you didn't come, so I know he's not real.'

Derek didn't care that he was lying. He just wanted to hurt as much as he could.

'I appreciated your friendship while I had it,' he wrote. 'You are the closest friend I ever had. Everyone else has rejected me all my life. I guess that's why it hurts so much that you're rejecting me, now. Good bye, Blaze. Goodbye, hopelessness. Goodbye, world.'

Derek read back over what he had written. With a satisfied nod, he placed it on the kitchen table. Without looking back, he headed out onto the street. His anger was too intense to feel any fear about the finality of what he was about to do. He didn't need to think about his plan for this night when he was finally brave enough to carry it out.

Chapter Eleven

Blaze settled on the lounge to watch the late news. There was no way he could sleep now. His heart and mind were too full of joy. Bonnie Blake had agreed to be his wife! So many years ago he had debated with the popular teenager and prayed for her salvation, offending and driving her away in the process. He had given up, but God had heard his heart's cry and changed Bonnie's life in a way Blaze never could.

He smiled to himself as he remembered Bonnie's haphazard attitude toward life and the way she had so often embarrassed him with her playful teasing. It was true she was now scarred from burns, but those burns were what had turned her to God. In Blaze's opinion, nothing could be more precious than that.

'My debating was useless,' he acknowledged to God, more than himself. 'It was you, in the end, who touched her heart. You are the one who changes lives. Thank you.'

Blaze's pleasant thoughts were interrupted as a news item caught his attention. The smile quickly vanished from his face and he leaned forward in the chair. There was a car racing through the city traffic, causing chaos as it went. Suddenly it screeched to a stop, allowing police cars to catch up. However, as soon as the police officers opened their doors, the car started up again. The driver was either drunk or didn't know how to drive. A four wheel drive veered out of the way only to swipe another vehicle side-on. Police cleared the roads ahead as much as possible, but watching, Blaze knew it couldn't end well.

'The teenager finally lost control of the stolen car and slammed into a power pole, losing his life in the process,' the newsreader reported as the final scene was shown. 'His name has not yet been released.'

Blaze caught his breath in a gasp. How could a teenager feel life was so empty? What would drive someone to do that? He turned off the television, his heart renewed with the burden to reach the hurting young people of the area.

***

Beauty awoke to a loud knocking on the door. Lazily, she turned to look at her alarm clock. Just after six. Who would come at this hour? And where was Blaze? Throwing on her dressing gown, she came to the door. A dishevelled woman stood there. Her eyes were red, either from drinking or crying.

'This where Blaze Clements lives?' Her demanding voice evidenced many years of smoking and Beauty glared at her. Didn't this woman know what time it was?

'I said, is this Blaze Clements' house?'

This time Beauty knew the woman had been drinking. The smell of alcohol wafted through the door.

Blaze came out of his room at that moment and it was clear he hadn't slept well. He glanced at Beauty, then faced the woman. 'Can I help you?'

'You Blaze?'

'Yes.'

'Where's my son?'

Blaze frowned, and Beauty wondered if she should phone the police. This woman was obviously drunk and confused.

'I don't know your son.' Blaze's voice was reassuring, but he didn't reach to open the door and invite the woman in the way he normally would.

'No?' The woman shoved a piece of paper toward Blaze. 'Explain this!'

Blaze peered through the screen door at the letter. Beauty looked over his shoulder, taking in the untidy scrawl and then seeing the name at the bottom.

Derek.

'Is he missing?' Blaze's voice was calm, but Beauty saw his shoulders stiffen and his eyes became troubled. Something was way wrong here.

'Missing? He's more than missing. He's probably dead and you killed him.'

Beauty expected Blaze to send the crazy woman on her way, but instead, he opened the door and asked her inside. Beauty kept a careful eye on the woman. She realised at that moment that she truly loved her brother and that if this woman did anything to hurt him, she would be there in an instant.

The woman refused to sit down while Blaze took the letter from her hand and began to read. As he read, Beauty watched the way his shoulders began to slump and an expression of defeat overtook him. When he looked up she recognised the look in his eyes. It mirrored a feeling she knew all too well. Guilt. Deep, unredeemable guilt that was weighing his heart down like lead.

Blaze finally spoke and his words came out in a hoarse whisper. 'I think maybe you should take this to the police.'

'Too right, I will.' The woman snatched the letter from his hand. 'And you, my friend, will be tried for murder! You and all you other crazy religious fanatics who pretend to care but drive people to suicide.'

Blaze shook his head as he sank further into the lounge chair. He didn't move as the woman let herself out the door. He didn't even seem to notice as Beauty came and sat beside him. Tentatively, she put a hand on his arm.

'Blaze?'

Finally he looked up and groaned, the pain in his expression making her want to weep. 'I was so happy, Beauty. It was all too good to be true. Bonnie agreed to be my wife! But now … now I've killed Derek.'

'What do you mean?' Beauty's heart beat faster at the look of intense pain on her brother's face. She had never seen him this way before and it scared her.

'He called last night and wanted to talk. I wouldn't and he went out and killed himself.'

'How do you know? He might not have carried out his threat.'

Blaze just shook his head, while Beauty stared at him helplessly.

'It's not your fault,' she tried again, but Blaze didn't seem to hear. She wrung her hands in frustration. Why should it be his fault? And how dare Derek suggest he killed himself because Blaze decided to go out for a night with Bonnie? It was crazy!

'Blaze.' She tried again, but he just turned absently and told her to go to school. Beauty knew he needed to be left alone, so with a heavy heart, went to get herself some breakfast.

Chapter Twelve

By the evening it was confirmed that Derek Sheen had taken his life in the stolen car.

'A teenager driven to death by negligence of his church minister,' the news reported. Blaze stared at the television, his face an expression of anguish. Beauty hardly knew what to say or do to help.

'Blaze, you can't take this on yourself. You heard Bonnie this afternoon. It was Derek's choice.'

Blaze didn't seem to hear as his head sank into his hands. Muffled words came from his mouth and Beauty strained to hear. 'Perhaps I was never meant to be a leader. Perhaps I rushed in too quickly and now other people are paying with their lives.'

'Blaze, stop it!' Beauty could hardly bear it. Mr Mathison had been around that afternoon and spent time in prayer with Blaze, but even that hadn't seemed to help. Usually the first to call out to God in his distress, Blaze had been strangely silent. Beauty had listened from the next room, expecting Blaze to pray at any moment, but he hadn't. In some ways, Beauty thought she understood. Voicing his guilt and pain would only concrete the reality in Blaze's mind

Much to Beauty's relief, Bonnie had arrived and Blaze smiled for the first time all day. Bonnie had shed tears of her own, but still Blaze's eyes were dry. And now, in the quietness of the evening Blaze was watching the news, letting it eat away at his heart. Beauty knew she had to do something. She had to shake him out of this. Noisily, she stretched and yawned. 'Well, I'm off to a party.'

No reaction. Blaze didn't even seem to hear.

'It's at Nate's place. He's having a party and a few of his mates are coming over.'

Nothing.

'Don't know when I'll be back.'

Blaze looked up, but then he just nodded and watched her go. Helplessness turned to anger as Beauty slammed the door behind her. It was as though she wasn't even there. She would take advantage of the situation and go out and enjoy herself.

Anything to get her mind off the drama going on at home.

It was easier than she had expected. Nate noticed her the moment she arrived and weaved his way through the crowded hallway, drink in hand. His eyes wandered over her graceful figure and he smiled, setting her at ease.

'Want one?' He handed her the drink and she took it. She needed something right now. Anything to numb the pain. She took a sip and tried not to react. It burned. But the pain in her heart burned deeper. Nate put an arm around her and led her into another room where bodies tussled for room to dance. Beauty took in a deep breath but coughed as cigarette smoke filled her lungs. Nate smiled at her apologetically. 'Let's find a quieter room.'

Enjoying the relaxing effect the alcohol was having on her mind and body, Beauty nodded and followed him into the living room. The music was a bit quieter, the room less crowded. Nate pushed one of the lounge chairs against the wall and held his hand out to her. 'Dance with me?'

She put her empty glass down on the coffee table. Dance was one thing she could do. In fact, she could dance with expert rhythm and grace on the back of a cantering horse.

At first Nate was the only one who noticed her gift, but soon others were beginning to watch from the corner of their eyes while continuing to dance.

'She's good.' The comments increased as one by one, people

stopped dancing to watch. Nate was having a hard time keeping up, his face becoming red and his breathing fast. It amused Beauty to see him try so hard to keep his composure, but someone came to his rescue. Beauty heard the familiar voice before she saw him. Chappy Eldwin. What was he doing here? She had avoided him since the pool barbeque but he clearly wasn't going to let her avoid him now.

'Excuse me. What's going on here?' He had put on an unnaturally deep voice and was walking in his Charlie Chaplin walk. People began to move toward them with smiles of amusement. With Chappy joining in, there would be double the entertainment.

'Excuse me, sir!' Chappy tapped Nate on the shoulder with a comically serious expression on his face. 'I think I can take it from here.'

Nate grinned and stepped aside while Beauty's face grew warm and she stopped still.

'No, don't stop!' Chappy took her by the waist. Immediately, he began to copy her moves with extreme clumsiness while the growing audience shouted with laughter. To Beauty's own surprise, she began to enjoy herself as she performed more and more difficult moves ranging from backflips to splits and somersaults which left the audience spellbound. The dramatic frown on Chappy's face grew deeper as his arms and legs seemed to become more tangled up in one another. Beauty couldn't help thinking he was a much more gifted clown than Banksie from the circus had ever been. Banksie had had to prepare performances to be a clown, but Chappy seemed to have a natural gift and came up with his acts on the spur of the moment.

Finally, he collapsed in a heap on the floor while everyone, including Beauty, laughed and clapped.

'Thank you Madam!' he gasped at Beauty. His eyes were sparkling, his mouth upturned in its usual smile. Why did he make her feel so awkward and yet so warm inside? She struggled to believe he saw her as nothing more than a charity case when he looked at her like that. He reached out his hand for her to help him up and she did so, then pulled back as though burned when his warm, strong fingers wrapped around hers. Where was Nate? She glanced around the room, unexplained panic filling her. Without another word to Chappy, she slipped through the crowd.

Nate was nowhere to be seen. She moved from room to room, scanning the crowds for his face. She stopped in the kitchen where a group of girls were colouring one another's hair. They looked up in interest as she entered and one patted a spare chair.

'Your turn?'

Beauty hesitated. Why not? Her dark hair fitted Beauty Clements, but she was Amy now.

The girl held some bottles out for her to look at. 'What colour?'

Beauty considered a moment before pointing to the mahogany. She had always liked the look of the photos of her mother with the natural reddish tinge to her hair. It was much more interesting than her own dark brown.

The girl began work and Beauty relaxed. It was nice to sit back and let someone else do her hair. However, the conversation around her was concerning. Drugs were clearly a part of these parties. And the way the girls spoke about the boys and their experiences with them sounded trashy. Beauty wasn't sure that she really belonged here, either. The moment her hair was finished she stood and left. Nate had to be around somewhere.

Finally Beauty gave up looking and stopped in the rumpus room, relieved to see Dee's familiar face at the billiard table.

'Hey, Amy, I saw you earlier. Where'd you learn to dance like that?'

Beauty smiled in response. 'On the back of a horse.' They group laughed, clearly believing she was joking. The laughter relaxed her again.

'Do you play pool as well?' one of the young men asked as he handed her a pool cue.

'No, you can't fit a table on the back of a horse.' It was a stupid thing to say, but the group had been drinking too much and laughed hysterically. Beauty smiled, appreciating the acceptance laughter brought. She was handed another drink as she took the offered pool cue. Her crazy remarks made less and less sense every time she missed the ball, but still the people around her laughed and she continued to drink. The longer she played, the harder it was to focus on the billiard balls, but she and the people around her were enjoying themselves.

Nate finally appeared from nowhere and handed her another drink. He put a protective arm around her waist. 'Having a good time?'

She tried to answer but struggled. She was feeling dizzier by the moment.

'Want to dance again?' Nate drew her away from her new-found billiard friends, but she could only shake her head. He shrugged and she watched as he approached another girl and began to dance with her. It wasn't that Beauty lacked fitness or the desire to dance. She just didn't feel well. She sank into the corner, her head in her hands.

'What are you doing?' Beauty hardly heard the familiar voice. She looked up into Chappy Eldwin's concerned face. It was the first time she remembered seeing him without his cheerful smile.

She let out a moan as she tried to focus on him. 'I feel pretty rotten.'

He reached a hand to pull her up. 'Here, let me take you home.'

'I can't go home.' She didn't even bother to look at his hand.

'Why not?'

'Blaze will be so disappointed in me.'

He sat down on the floor beside her. 'I think he would prefer you to go home like this than stay out and make him worry.'

'He won't worry. He didn't even notice …' she began, but it was too hard to keep talking.

'I know Blaze and he will be worried,' Chappy argued gently.

Beauty just shook her head, wishing she had never accepted any of the drinks. It was true, she had been relaxed, the life of the party. But was it worth it?

Chappy lifted her to her feet, allowing her to lean against him.

There was something about Chappy that was different tonight. He was so serious, but there was something in his eyes. Something deep and almost tender. Or was it just that she was drunk?

'Come on,' he encouraged as they made their way down the dark footpath and toward Beauty's home. 'We're almost there.'

Beauty felt the warmth of his arm around her and drew in a deep breath. Why was he doing this? Why did he care? 'Chappy, why …'

He was listening, looking at her and waiting patiently. She sighed in frustration. If she wasn't drunk she'd be able to get the words out. But then again, if she wasn't drunk she probably wouldn't have the courage to ask him.

They were at the front door. Blaze was there; she could make out his fuzzy outline.

'I'm sorry, Blaze. I should have brought her earlier.'

Chappy's tone told Beauty that Blaze was indeed upset to see her in this state. She heard him open the screen door and then felt Blaze's strong arm around her as he drew her in. His deep voice rumbled from somewhere above her.

'It's not your fault, Chappy. I wasn't thinking straight when I let her go out. It's been a long day.'

Blaze helped her onto the lounge and Beauty moaned as she lay there. She would never touch another drink in her life!

But what was Chappy doing? Why wasn't he going home? He was sitting across from Blaze and studying his youth leader with a worried expression. 'Blaze, what's happened?' Chappy's voice was genuinely concerned and Beauty knew then that there was a whole lot more to Chappy Eldwin than met the eye.

To her relief, she heard Blaze begin telling Chappy about Derek. She wanted to hear more, but she was dozing off. Vaguely, she heard Chappy pray. And then Blaze. Blaze was praying again! Thanks, God! Why thanks, God? Did she even believe in God? She couldn't finish the thought before she fell asleep again.

***

Bonnie awoke with Blaze and Beauty on her heart. She needed to pray. Yet even after pouring her heart out to God, she felt she needed to do more. It was only six in the morning, so maybe if she got up now she would have time to call on them before she headed off to uni lectures for the day.

When Blaze opened the door, she knew why God had put them on her heart. Beauty was lying on the lounge, bucket by her side and looking terrible. Her hair was limp and had clearly been coloured the night before. Blaze didn't look much better than his sister. His face was drawn, his eyes still full of sorrow. He nodded toward Beauty.

'She went to a party last night. I didn't really notice when she left.' His whisper sounded strained as he fell into a chair with a defeated sigh. 'She drank and now she feels sick. She won't talk to me and she won't get up. She's got school …'

Bonnie glanced back at Beauty who was being sick again. 'I think school is out of the question for today.'

Blaze gave a weary sigh. 'She probably can't remember much about last night and she's probably frightened, but if she'd just talk to me about it.'

'Let me talk to her,' Bonnie offered, while Blaze just nodded.

'Go ahead. You're a female. You know how she thinks.'

Bonnie doubted anyone knew how Beauty thought, but she was willing to give it a try. She came to the lounge and sat, moving a strand of mahogany coloured hair from Beauty's clammy forehead. 'How are you?'

Beauty blinked at her, then held her stomach and moaned. 'As well as I deserve to be. But that's what I get for trying to be someone else.'

'Is that why you drank? To help you enjoy the party?'

Beauty shook her head. 'No, just to try to be nice. But I'm not nice, so I might as well give up if alcohol is the only way I can be who I want to be.'

75

'But Beauty, it must be who you really are somewhere inside.' Bonnie tried to hide her surprise at Beauty's vulnerability. She had expected to be met with sarcasm or anger, not this willingness to talk. 'You're always pretending and covering up how you really feel. You have pain you won't let yourself forget. Drinking helped you forget.'

'What would you know?' Beauty moaned again. 'You have everything, Bonnie Blake. You have no idea about real pain. And Blaze didn't either until yesterday.'

With that, Beauty rolled her face into the lounge and refused to respond any further. Bonnie left the room, deep in thought. What did Beauty Clements consider real pain to be? If the agony of being seriously burned in a fire and being rejected because of her scars was not real pain, what was? 'Lord, help me understand.' Then it dawned on her. Beauty believed she had caused a death. She knew Blaze was struggling over what had happened to Derek, but it hadn't occurred to her that Beauty was living with the same guilt. Maybe she really did care that the little boy had been killed when his car hit her horse.

Chapter Thirteen

Beauty made her way quietly through the house, wishing every step didn't aggravate her headache. Blaze had a meeting with the high school chaplains and wouldn't be home until lunchtime. She had the house to herself.

Gingerly, she made her way through each room until she came to the room Blaze called his studio. Filled with all his paintings, the room fascinated her. Although she had turned down Blaze's offer to show her his art work in the past, Beauty now took the opportunity to see what she had missed. Squinting her eyes against her headache, she began to look around.

She had to admit each finished piece was very good, as good as the painting of Montford Express. Her eyes wandered to the easel standing by the window and she made her way over. Stunned by what she saw, Beauty stared at the unfinished painting before her.

'That's us,' she whispered, looking at the family painting. 'And that's Mum with her arms around me and Storm.' She studied the face of her mother. Blaze had put such joy in her eyes and those eyes were looking directly at her. It looked like any normal, happy family and they were all laughing and smiling. Beauty reached a hand, about to touch the picture, when she realised it might not be dry. Blaze must never know she had seen his painting nor that she had thought of touching it.

'He understands,' she muttered to herself, unable to draw her eyes away as she backed toward the door. 'He still thinks about

Mum.' For the first time in years she felt a connection to her brother. He understood and felt what she felt. And he knew they were all important – her mother, her, every one of them.

She was about to turn away when her eye caught the paint brush by the easel and the tube of white oil paint. What if …? Her mind raced. She didn't know how to paint, not really, but Blaze had suggested she fix the painting of Montford Express. Could she do it? She moved back into the room and snatched up the brush and tube of paint before she could change her mind.

It took a good fifteen minutes for Beauty to gather up the courage to touch the canvas with the brush, but once she began she felt she was bringing Montford Express back to life. Love and grief overwhelmed her as she tenderly moved the brush back and forth, touching up the colours, shaping the white markings into what they should have been. Finally finished, she reached a sleeve to wipe her face and found her cheeks wet and streaming with tears.

She found the unfamiliar tears confusing and frightening. What was happening to her? Was she losing control, and what would happen if she did? Afraid to find out, she pulled herself together, washed out the paint brush and returned them to Blaze's studio, refusing to look at the painting again.

When Blaze arrived home, Beauty heard him wander back into his studio and resume work on his painting. She longed to come and watch, but pride kept her at a distance. She would wait until he went out again that afternoon.

She heard his footsteps heading toward her room and quickly lay back on her bed and closed her eyes. The headache had gone, but the last thing she wanted was to be sent to school. She needed to look sick. When Blaze poked his head in her room she opened her eyes. His were filled with concern. 'Are you okay?'

She nodded.

'I've got an appointment …'

So he didn't really care. He just had to leave again and needed to let her know. 'I'll be okay. You go and do your little counselling thing.'

'It's called pastoral care.'

'Whatever.'

As soon as he left the house, Beauty crept into Blaze's studio to where the easel stood. She had to see her mother one more time, alive and well in Blaze's painting. The picture on the canvas made her feel as though her mother wasn't completely gone - that an important part of her still existed.

Beauty felt disappointment knife through her as she looked. The picture was no longer beautiful or realistic, for etched across its was one word, 'Guilt'.

Anger filled her. 'What's he doing? He's ruined it.' With that, she turned away, determined never to look at Blaze's work again.

Her annoyance diminished when he arrived home late, shoulders slumped and face downcast. He had a lot going on right now. He couldn't be blamed for ruining his painting in a few irrational brushstrokes. It seemed she was right. Guilt was eating away at him. She would try to be considerate.

'How was your meeting?'

He looked confused. 'Meeting?'

'The one you went to this afternoon. Your pastoral care thing.'

'Oh, that.' He got himself a glass and filled it with water. 'It wasn't actually a meeting.' He took a long, slow drink and she waited. Finally he put down the glass and sighed. 'I saw a lawyer.'

'A lawyer? What for?'

His shrug didn't make him look nonchalant the way he clearly hoped it would. 'Derek's mother is trying to sue me for negligence. She reckons I should have been charged with manslaughter.'

'Manslaughter? Negligence?' Beauty's eyes sparked with indignation. 'How does she think she can get away with that? She didn't even have custody of her son!'

'True.' Blaze nodded, 'But she wants to sue his father as well.'

'That's ridiculous!' Beauty fumed, then stopped at the look in Blaze's eyes. 'You do understand that it's crazy, don't you?'

When he didn't answer, she came toward him. 'Blaze, it's not your fault. What Derek did was his own choice.' Even as she spoke the words, she thought of her mother, of Bonnie's burns, of Blaze's tetanus and of the little boy who had been killed the night Monty died. But they were her fault, weren't they? A voice somewhere inside dared her to hope she could someday be free of guilt, but she knew the truth. With a shake of her head she turned from Blaze. They were all her fault and nothing could ever change the fact.

Although Beauty had determined not to look at Blaze's paintings anymore, curiosity drove her into his studio only a few days later. Her heart beat hard in her chest as she approached the easel, wondering what she would find. She visibly relaxed when she saw that the old picture wasn't there. It seemed Blaze was working on a new one. A large, realistic wooden cross filled the canvas. She looked closer. Hidden within the cross was another picture. It was then that she realised. This was the very same picture she had been looking at the day before, only the word 'guilt' was now overshadowed by the cross. Shaking her head, Beauty walked from the room. Blaze hadn't been thinking of her or her mother at all. All he could think about was his own beliefs about life and death.

As she lay in bed that night, the image on Blaze's canvas continued to plague her. She had been the cause of her mother leaving their family and all the pain her family had been through. The guilt was hers. Blaze had often tried to explain to her how Jesus took all wrongdoing when He died on the cross, so that anyone who accepted that could live free of guilt. So if Blaze truly believed that and understood it, why was he blaming himself for Derek's death when he could be forgiven?

'He can apply religion to everyone else, but doesn't know how to live it himself,' she muttered as she drifted off to sleep. 'He's too busy looking after everyone else to see he has needs of his own.'

Beauty returned to school the next day, surprised that Blaze hadn't even mentioned her drunken state after the party. He seemed preoccupied with Derek's death.

She fumbled through science, watching other students set up a tripod and Bunsen burner. She had never done it before but wasn't about to admit it. Dee made it look so easy, the way she turned on the gas then lit the burner and sat it beneath the tripod, its blue flame burning steadily. Carefully, Beauty turned on the gas. Then she pulled the tripod and Bunsen burner from the cupboard and sat them on the desk. Time to light. Holding her breath, she did so, then jumped back as a great whoof of flame burst out at her then died. Quickly she turned off the gas. First lesson learned: don't turn the gas on too early.

'Having trouble?'

Danielle was looking over at her, her expression mocking. Beauty didn't bother to answer as she prepared to start again. The class had a practical science assessment tomorrow and she had to get this right.

This time she couldn't even get a flame. There had to be a balance in there somewhere, but she needed to work it out without her class watching. She would come in during the lunch break. Glancing at the laboratory roster, she saw that no seniors had booked in for lunchtime. She would sneak in and experiment until she got it to work.

It was no trouble getting away from Dee and her friends that lunchtime once she gave a simple explanation that she needed to go to the library. Once inside the empty science laboratory, Beauty began to feel relaxed. Now she could work things out for herself without the pressure of other people's judging eyes.

She smiled, kicked off her shoes at the door and headed over to the bench. She knew the rules about wearing covered shoes for science, but it wasn't like she was going to be using acid or glass. She was simply going to get that Bunsen burner alight without any sudden explosions. She would do it calmly and smoothly, the way Dee always managed.

Reaching down into the cupboard, Beauty enjoyed the cool floor beneath her feet. That was one thing she missed about the circus – being free to wander around without shoes. Moving a flask to the side, she reached in to where the burner sat. However, as she dragged it out, its plastic tubing caught against the flask, causing it to crash to the floor. Beauty managed to jump out of the way just before it shattered, then stood staring in horror at the mess before her.

'You're as bad as Misty!' she scolded herself, speaking of her clumsy older sister, 'but at least Misty is likeable.'

Glancing around, Beauty knew she couldn't risk walking through the glass to get a broom and dust pan with bare feet. She'd have to walk across the bench tops to reach the door and collect her shoes.

Just as she stood on the bench top, the door to the lab slowly opened. Horrified, she stopped still. Was someone else sneaking in like she had? The person walked in. Chappy Eldwin. He didn't see her at first, but when he looked up a slow smile broke across his face.

'Is this a usual practice of yours?' He chuckled up at her reddened face then glanced to the shattered glass on the floor.

'What?' She tried to look indignant.

'Standing on science lab benches during lunchtime with no shoes on?'

Beauty said nothing while Chappy made his way over to her.'Want me to carry you safely to the door?'

'No!' She moved to the other side of the bench, ignoring his playful grin. There was no way she was going to let him touch her. 'You could bring me my shoes.'

He nodded and went to get them, still chuckling. 'You know it's against the rules to be in here on your own.' He held her shoes out to her.

'Speak for yourself.' Beauty took her shoes from his outstretched hand then sat down on the edge of the bench to do up her laces.

'I have permission.'

Beauty glanced at him wishing he wouldn't look at her that way. There was that tenderness in his expression again. She preferred it when he was clowning around, not at risk of getting to close to her heart. 'Whose permission?'

'Mr Rush asked me to come and see if he left his notebook in here. I can come back and stay in here with you until you've finished what you're doing. Then you won't get into trouble.'

'Don't worry about it. I'm about to leave anyway.' Beauty didn't like the way she snapped, but she needed to hide her discomfort. She couldn't let him see the way he affected her. Jumping down, she moved past him to find a broom and dustpan. Chappy pointed to the corner of the room where one sat and she nodded her thanks. He watched as she swept up the shards of glass, then brought her a piece of newspaper to wrap them. He pointed to a yellow lidded bin. 'They go in there.'

'Thanks. I'm going now.'

Chappy shrugged. 'Okay.'

She was aware of the way he watched her leave and heard the chuckle escape his lips. Frustration overwhelmed her. She would never get used to the world outside the circus. There were so many unspoken rules that left her in awkward situations. She just wanted to be out riding Montford Express, free once more to be herself. Whoever she was. She didn't really know. Chappy didn't seem to know either, but it appeared that he liked her anyway. She would never understand Chappy Eldwin.

Chapter Fourteen

Blaze sat beside his lawyer, unable to bring himself to look up. Derek's parents and their respective lawyers sat across from them, silent and expectant. Someone began tapping a pen on the desk and Blaze hoped Mr Mathison would hurry up. He was supposed to be here by now. He breathed a sigh of relief as the door opened and Mr Mathison walked in. He gave Blaze a friendly smile then looked directly at Derek's parents. 'Sorry to keep you waiting. I called this meeting because I think we can save a lot of legal costs and court time.'

Mr Mathison sat down beside Blaze and leaned his elbows on the table. Derek's mother narrowed her eyes while his father shuffled uncomfortably. Mr Sheen looked older than ever, but there was an openness in his expression that relieved Blaze. Perhaps he would be willing to hear Mr Mathison out.

'Now, I know some people believe Blaze Clements is the one to blame for your son's death, but I would say that Derek wanted to take his last chance to make an impact on this world.'

Derek's father nodded, but his mother made no response. Mr Mathison leaned forward, resting his arms on the desk, his gaze almost challenging. 'So he picked the most compassionate man he knew. He picked the one least worthy of blame and lashed out at him with all his strength. Don't the words in his letter show how much he knew Blaze cared? And don't Derek's careless actions in that stolen car show how little he cared who he might hurt? You know, I believe that of all those involved in Derek's life, Blaze is the least to blame.

At least he tried to help Derek.'

Complete silence filled the room, until Derek's father looked Blaze in the eye and swallowed hard. 'Thank you for being a friend to my son.'

Derek's mother jumped up. 'Hey, what about the note? This is the man who ignored Derek's cry for help, remember? All the evidence is against him!'

'Actually, no it isn't.'

This time it was Blaze's lawyer speaking. 'Blaze can't be held criminally responsible for Derek's choice, no matter what the note says.'

Derek's mother turned to her lawyer. 'That's not true. Tell them it's not true.'

Her lawyer steadily met her gaze. 'It is true.'

'But why didn't you tell me? Why let this minister come in here and quote all his garbage when you could have just told me?'

Her lawyer looked away for a moment, then back. 'Because Mr Mathison hoped you would understand that Blaze is not responsible whether or not there is a criminal case here.'

Derek's mother's eyes narrowed. 'You wanted me to make this poor excuse for a youth minister feel better about himself? To ease his guilt? Well I'm sorry, but there is no way I'm ever going to do that.' She looked down her nose at Mr Sheen. 'And as for you, I thought you'd stand by me. I thought you loved Derek. But I'm not giving up that easily.'

'Mrs Sheen, you are free to continue, of course, but these are the fees if you lose.' Her lawyer pushed a sheet of paper in front of her and her eyes widened before she glared at Blaze. 'Well I might not be able to sue, but I can let all the TV stations know about this.'

With that, she stormed from the room. Blaze's lawyer shook his head. 'They won't take it on. They know the legal implications and it won't get anywhere.'

Blaze frowned. 'So that's it?'

Mr Sheen's lawyer nodded. 'Yes, legally, that's it.'

∗∗∗

'How did today go?' Bonnie asked when Blaze arrived at her door that evening. For the first time in days, he smiled and Bonnie felt the burden in her own heart lift.

He settled onto the lounge and reached for her. 'I'm not going to be sued. Derek's father doesn't blame me. He recognises that Derek had problems of his own. And his mother reluctantly agreed to drop the case because she can't afford to pay the solicitors fees if there's any chance she could lose.'

Bonnie smiled as she snuggled in beside him. These last few days had been so hard for Blaze, but now it seemed he had finished blaming himself for the whole tragedy. She rubbed a thumb across his hand. 'So now we can put it all behind us.'

'I feel like death has been my every thought ever since it happened.' Blaze shook his head. 'Now I want to remember I'm alive and focus on the living.'

'Like me,' Bonnie teased. 'I've been feeling a bit neglected lately.'

Immediately she recognised her mistake as she saw Blaze's face cloud over and his body stiffen. Why had she teased him with those words? The last thing she wanted was to remind him of Derek's accusations of neglect. She knew then that it would be a while before she had the old Blaze Clements back. Until that time, she would have to measure every word carefully.

∗∗∗

Blaze ached to attend Derek's funeral although he knew it was unwise. There was no need to antagonise Derek's mother by showing up. He knew she would be bitterly telling everyone about her beloved son driven to suicide by a church minister. For the first time Blaze saw that Derek's deceit matched his mother's. Anger welled up inside him. *He deliberately set out to hurt me.* Just as quickly, he shook the thought away. He shouldn't try to transfer his guilt to Derek. That wasn't fair. Derek was the victim. He would have to shut away the anger he felt toward Derek and always remember that the whole tragedy would not have happened had he not insisted on spending a night out with Bonnie.

Thinking of that night, he suddenly remembered Danielle had called earlier, saying she needed to talk. He jumped up from the lounge and turned off the television. 'So much for not letting it happen again.' His fingers weren't altogether steady as he dialled her number. She took way too long to answer. Finally he heard her voice. He caught his breath, trying to steady his hands. 'Danielle? It's Blaze.'

'Blaze, thanks for calling back. I just needed to talk. I'm really confused.' She began telling him about her latest argument with Chappy and Blaze listened attentively, offering advice and sympathy. After all, it was he that she had sought, just like Derek had.

***

'Danielle rang last night,' Blaze told Bonnie the next day. 'She's having trouble with Chappy again.'

Bonnie smiled, knowing Danielle's little tiffs with Chappy were becoming more frequent. 'Do you want me to ring and talk to her?'

'It's okay. She seemed a lot happier after I talked with her.'

Bonnie's brows lifted in surprise. 'But Blaze, it was your day off.' She didn't dare mention again their agreement to let her deal with the females in the youth gorup.

'I know. But remember Derek.'

'I thought you had stopped blaming yourself.' Bonnie's disappointment went deep.

'I have, but I've also learned from my mistake.'

'Mistake? Doesn't mistake mean you are still blaming yourself?'

'No! I'm just admitting I did wrong, accepting Christ's forgiveness and making sure it doesn't happen again.' His tone had become defensive and Bonnie had no response. She wished she could understand why Blaze's words bothered her so deeply.

As they sat in silence, Beauty passed through the lounge room

87

'I'm going out.'

Blaze jumped up. 'Wait a minute!'

She looked back. 'Yeah?'

'Where are you going?'

'Just to a party.'

'I thought we had an agreement, Beauty. You always tell me where you're going.'

'I did tell you.' Beauty was clearly taken aback by Blaze's fierce tone and Bonnie felt her body tense, ready for conflict. This was a Blaze she hadn't come across before; one she didn't know how to handle.

'If you had told me, I'd know where you're going.' Blaze's voice was harsh as he came toward Beauty, eyes dark. 'You haven't even told me who you're going with.'

'Alright, alright! Keep calm.' Beauty glared at her brother. He towered over her, but her own expression was just as determined as his. 'I'm going out with Nate as usual and we're not sure where yet.'

'Well, you're not going until I know where.' Blaze took a step forward, but Beauty had already left, slamming the door behind her. Slowly, Blaze came back and sank onto the lounge while Bonnie tried to mask her shock. He had always been so reasonable with his sister in the past. Clearly, the whole Derek incident was bothering him more than he cared to talk about. She was about to ask him about it when the phone rang and he jumped up and disappeared to answer it. He returned a few minutes later. 'That was Reece. He needs advice about what course to take for uni. I said I'd go over there.'

'Now?'

He nodded, his expression apologetic. 'I might be a while, so I'll catch up with you later.' With that, he disappeared out the door.

Bonnie stared after him. What was she supposed to do? She had no idea if he was expecting her to go home or to wait here for him to return. She had no key to his house, so she couldn't lock it up if she left. There was nothing to do but to sit alone and wait for him.

It was Beauty who arrived home first to find Bonnie asleep on the lounge.

'What are you doing here?' Her words were slurred, a tell-tale sign that she had been drinking again.

'Waiting for Blaze. He had to go and see someone.' Bonnie glanced at the clock. She had been asleep for hours.

'And he left you here alone?' Beauty was incredulous. 'Great boyfriend!'

Bonnie said nothing.

'Why didn't you go home?' Beauty asked after a few minutes, blinking as though trying to clear her vision.

'I don't have a key to lock up with.'

Beauty took a key from her pocket and threw it on the table.

'Did you have a good night?' Bonnie ventured cautiously as Beauty made her way to the window and gazed out. Beauty didn't answer, but her expression was pained. Bonnie wished she would speak what was on her troubled mind. Suddenly she got her wish.

'Nate's wrong! I can't live for myself.' Beauty cried, turning dark eyes to Bonnie.

'What are you talking about?' Bonnie was confused. Surely Beauty wasn't suicidal?

'I have to live for my mum! I killed her and now I have to make up for that.'

Bonnie stared at Beauty in shock. 'What do you mean you killed her?'

'I just did.'

'How?'

Beauty swallowed, and for the first time, Bonnie saw her cry. 'Just by being born.'

Beauty broke down and wept. When Bonnie came to her side, she jumped up and rushed to her room, while Bonnie stared after her, dumbstruck.

'What a night,' she muttered, then packed her things to go home. She picked up the key Beauty had thrown on the table and quietly let herself out, locking the door behind her.

Chapter Fifteen

Beauty didn't answer the door. Let whoever it was keep knocking. Probably a sales person. She sighed and switched the TV channel. The knocking came again. Could they hear the television? Or maybe Blaze had told someone he'd be here and forgotten again. He was so distant and vague these days. Imagine leaving his fiancée here the night before with no way to lock up and go home! These days she wondered if Bonnie was really special to him at all.

The knock came again. It was getting annoying. Her hangover from the night before hadn't quite gone and the knocking was irritating her. Might as well deal with it and send the caller away. Annoyed, she yanked open the door and came face to face with Bonnie's confused frown.

'Where's Blaze?'

'He didn't tell you?' Beauty's brows raised.

'Tell me what?'

'Danielle's father broke his leg and they needed someone to mow their lawn.'

Bonnie said nothing, but it was clear she was trying to control her emotions. Then she looked squarely at Beauty. 'Will you tell him I called? And ask him to call me when he's ready to prepare for Bible study?'

Beauty's eyes widened. 'That's right. You do that every Wednesday afternoon.'

Bonnie shrugged. 'I guess he forgot.'

'I guess so. Again.' Beauty's words were pointed and Bonnie jarred for a moment before turning away. Her acceptance of the situation annoyed Beauty. Why was Bonnie so placid all the time? Didn't anything upset her? 'Hey, you're not just going, are you? Don't you have anything else for me to tell him?'

Bonnie turned back. 'Like what?'

'Like, if you're going to take me for granted, find someone else.'

'What?' Bonnie's face was an expression of shock. 'No. No, nothing like that.'

Beauty shook her head. 'He's going to keep doing it if you keep letting him. You're so naive sometimes.'

'I'm naive?' Bonnie demanded, surprising Beauty with her anger. Maybe Bonnie did feel something after all.

'Yes. He was in love with you before, but it's worn off. Now he just sees the convenience of his relationship with you. You help him out and you give him the hope of a mother for his dear little niece, Sky.'

Bonnie came back toward the screen door, her eyes flashing. 'I'm not the one who needs to watch out, Beauty. You are!'

'What do you mean?'

'I mean you need to be careful. At least I can trust Blaze, but I've heard about your boyfriend, Nate, and he's a real lady's man. He may want more from you than you're willing to give.'

'What?' Beauty's surprise left her speechless for a moment. It seemed Bonnie did fight back if the right buttons were pushed. She shrugged, trying to appear nonchalant. 'I don't know what you're talking about.'

'I'm talking about his reputation. He's well known for what he wants from his girlfriends. Blaze might be too preoccupied to warn you, but I'm not.'

'Who told you that? You can't always believe everything you hear. I know Nate and he's not like that.'

Bonnie's glare faded. She shrugged in defeat, then stepped back away from the door. 'I'm just trying to warn you.'

'Well, I don't need it, thanks. I'm not going to follow in Prince's footsteps and have a child at sixteen if that's what you're worried about. I'm going to wait until I've lived my life a bit and am committed to someone.'

'I'm not just talking about deciding to have children, Beauty.'

Beauty rolled her eyes. 'I know that. There's something called protection, you know. Besides, I wouldn't be with anyone until I'm good and ready.'

With that, she slammed the door in Bonnie's face, not caring to admit that the words had bothered her. What did Nate really expect from her? She had no idea. One thing she did know – she would learn from her brother Prince's mistake and never allow herself to fall pregnant to someone she hadn't committed herself to. Another thing – she would make sure she was never taken for granted. Bonnie really should make Blaze see what he was doing. She should stand up for herself!

***

Danielle brought a drink out to Blaze. He stopped the mower and ran the back of his hand over his sweaty brow.

'Thanks.' He took a long drink, then looked up in surprise as Danielle's hand rested on his arm. Her eyes were tender.

'You're an amazing man, Blaze Clements. If I ever get married, I want to find someone just like you.'

Blaze smiled absently at her compliment as he wiped dirty hands down his shirt and moved away from her touch. 'What's this ever business?'

'I don't know.' She shrugged. 'Sometimes I just wonder if any man would really want me.' She glanced down at herself then looked back up to Blaze, her eyes wide and sad.

Blaze was confused. 'Why wouldn't they want you?'

'I don't know. I just keep worrying about my weight.'

Blaze tried not to roll his eyes. 'Why do girls do that?'

She let out a deep sigh. 'Because guys always go for the attractive,

92

slim ones. The plump ones are always left behind.'

Her look was so vulnerable that Blaze reached a gentle hand to rest on her shoulder. 'You're not overweight!' He glanced at her perfect figure, then away. He caught the slightest glimpse of a smile passing over her face before her expression became subdued and her tone plaintive.

'So why doesn't Chappy love me the way I am?'

'I can't imagine why,' Blaze answered without thought, then hearing the implication of his words, added, 'but I can assure you that God loves you the way you are.'

Danielle gave him a satisfied, beaming smile. Blaze knew he had unwittingly admitted he found her attractive. Disarmed for a moment, he longed to escape. Danielle's seductive nature was beginning to bother him. She was still gazing up at him with an adoring expression and it was getting awkward. He held the glass back out to her. 'I'd better get back to mowing.'

This time her expression was nothing short of flirty. 'But you've been working so hard. Every hard working man deserves some play time.'

She had made up his mind. 'Sorry, Danielle. I really better get back to work.' He restarted the mower as quickly as he could, aware of her eyes on him. Defeated, Danielle headed back inside, tightly holding the glass which had been in Blaze's hands only a few moments before. Blaze watched her, shaking his head. What was the girl playing at? She knew he was engaged to Bonnie. Bonnie!

He was supposed to be preparing Bible study with her this afternoon. He slammed off the mower while Danielle looked back at him in anticipation.

'Danielle, I've got to go.' His tone was urgent as he raced away, calling over his shoulder. 'I just remembered something. I'll be back later.'

He felt Danielle's eyes still on him as he jumped into his vehicle. He glanced back for only a second to see her smiling. He knew her smile might not have been so wide had she known the only one he cared about at that moment was his beloved Bonnie and how upset she must be.

'Bonnie?' Blaze asked breathlessly as he arrived home. He fumbled with his key and rushed in the door. Beauty looked up from the television program she was watching.

'She went home, thanks to you.'

'She did? Was she upset?'

'Upset enough to go off at me. She knows you just want her as a mother for Sky. I wouldn't bother going after her, if I was you.' Blaze didn't hear her out. He didn't slow down until he was walking down the path to Bonnie's front door. Anxiety began to beat a drum in his chest and he reached a tentative hand to ring the doorbell. It was Bonnie's mother who answered. She didn't even give him a chance to ask as she opened the front door. 'You'll find her out the back feeding the hens.'

He nodded and headed out the back. To his dismay, Bonnie sat beside the hen's yard, her head in her hands.

'Bonnie?' He didn't miss the way she tried to wipe her tears before she turned to attempt a smile at him.

'Bonnie, I'm so sorry.' Drawing her to him, he put both arms around her. 'I know I've been preoccupied. There's just been so much on my mind.'

'I know. It's okay.'

'No, it's not. I've made you cry.'

She shrugged. 'You're forgiven now you're here.' She gave him a watery smile, but he wasn't convinced.

'I think we should spend more time together.' He turned her to him and wiped her tears with his thumbs.

She gazed up him and her tears came faster. 'Beauty says you don't really care about me anymore. Blaze, I don't like the thought that you might be taking me for granted.'

He moaned. 'Oh, Bonnie, I'm so sorry. I love you so much and I miss the time we used to have together. Why don't we make a time to spend a whole day together?'

Her eyes brightened. 'I'd like that. When?'

'Well, I've arranged for Sky to come and stay with me for a few days, so I'm taking time off then.'

He stopped. Would she think he really did just want her as a mother for Sky? He tried again. 'Let's do it as soon as we can.'

Her big blue eyes were looking at him so trustingly it scared him. *Lord, help me stop letting her down. Help me love her deeply and completely – to be everything she needs.*

He ignored the still, small voice in his heart that warned him he couldn't do that for anyone. Only God could.

Chapter Sixteen

'Where are we going?' Beauty asked Nate, surprised as he led her away from the dance club.

He gave a vague wave of his hand. 'I have something special planned for us tonight.'

'Like what?'

He ignored her question as he gave her a smile. 'Where's the middle of your top?' She chuckled as he reached to touch the skin of her waist. 'You know it's not meant to be there.'

'I do,' he agreed with a laugh. 'And that's why I like this top. But I'd like it even better if it went higher.'

'Higher?' Beauty was beginning to feel uncomfortable. His look was too intense as he studied her shape.

'Yeah, like to the neckline.' He reached to pull her top up, but Beauty immediately pulled away.

Nate looked surprised and hurt. 'What's up?'

She glared. 'I just don't want you to touch me there, that's all.'

'Why not? Can't I even touch my girl without getting my head snapped off?'

Beauty's eyes narrowed as she remembered Bonnie's warning about Nate's reputation. 'Depends where and how you want to touch me.'

Nate chuckled coldly. 'You didn't care when you were drunk.'

Beauty blushed, confusion filling her. 'What do you mean?'

'I mean you were more than happy to sleep with me last night.'

Beauty began to feel sick. 'But I woke up at home.'

'Yes, but only because Chappy insisted on taking you. Reckoned he didn't want me taking advantage of you. I told him you would be just as willing to sleep with me when you were in your right mind, but it seems I was wrong.'

Beauty stared at Nate in horror. Surely he was lying, but his face told her otherwise.

Fear and shock fuelled her anger as she spat at him. 'As if I'd be willing to sleep with you! I'm not that type of girl. I don't throw myself on any man who asks me.'

Nate's eyes narrowed and his look scared her. 'So I'm any man now, am I? You let me buy you drinks, dance with you, help you fit in and then suddenly when I ask for a little something in return, you turn on me. You're a taker, Amy Clements. You have no idea how to love!'

With that, they began to swear and curse at one another, until Nate turned on his heel and stalked away. Beauty stared after his retreating figure, her eyes sparking with the intense anger she felt.

'I'm not a taker!' She stamped her foot. 'I just value my integrity.'

Thinking of Blaze and Bonnie, she felt proud of herself. They would not have any reason to be disappointed in her this time. But thinking of Chappy Eldwin, she moaned. Chappy knew she had been drunk and he knew what Nate had expected of her. Chappy Eldwin had rescued her once again.

Slowly, she began the walk home. Bonnie Blake had been right about Nate after all. He was only interested as long as there was a chance he could gain what he wanted from her.

'I'm not that kind of girl,' Beauty repeated, willing herself to believe it. But somewhere inside, a voice whispered that Nate must have had some reason to think she was.

***

'Sky, this is Bonnie,' Blaze told the little girl standing by his side. 'She's going to be your new mother when you come to live with me.'

At his words, the little girl's face lit into a brilliant smile. 'You are my mummy?'

Bonnie threw a desperate look in Blaze's direction. Blaze seemed unfazed.

'She will be.'

'Will you read me stories?' Sky said, her small face filled with an expression of hope and delight.

Bonnie forgot her own uncertainty. 'Of course.'

'And I will have a real mummy and daddy who live with me?'

When Blaze didn't step in, Bonnie shrugged and smiled. 'I guess so.'

The little girl ran to her new mother. Sky was responding to Bonnie with unveiled delight and admiration.

'I like you,' Sky kept telling Bonnie throughout the day and Bonnie wondered what she had been worried about. She didn't even have to win this little girl's affection. For some reason, she already had it. There was also something special about sitting beside Blaze, holding a little girl in her lap, and reading stories aloud. Blaze did his own share of reading and his love for his niece was so evident it brought a tightness to Bonnie's chest that she didn't understand. She just knew she was witnessing something special and unbreakable. She longed for the day when she, Blaze and Sky could be a true family.

'I don't want to go,' Sky cried, clinging to Blaze and Bonnie when her foster parents came to collect her late in the afternoon. A look passed between the foster parents and Blaze and Bonnie as they silently asked each other how to deal with this. Eventually is was Bonnie who removed the little girl's hands from around her leg and knelt down to look into her face.

'I don't want you to go, either,' she admitted, waiting until Sky's eyes met with hers. 'But you can come back soon. Until you do, how would you like to take home the books we read to you today so Aunty Shelley and Uncle Tom can read them to you?'

Sky still looked hesitant until her foster mother stepped forward.

'What a good idea. How about you go and get them, Sky, and I will read one to you as soon as we get home?'

Sky grinned up at Shelley, finally placated. All adults breathed a sigh of relief as she ran inside to collect the books and came out still smiling. She even managed a cheerful wave as the car drove out of sight. Bonnie felt the tightness in her chest again. How she longed to be a 'real' mother to that delightful little girl who meant so much to Blaze.

'Don't be fooled,' Beauty warned that night, after watching Sky's warm response to Bonnie. 'She's only a little girl now. She doesn't fully understand the impact of what she's doing. You wait until she's a teenager and discovers that Blaze only married you so you could be her mother. See what she thinks of you then.'

Bonnie shook her head at Beauty, wondering why the teenager was in such a foul mood. It had begun yesterday and was persisting a little longer than Bonnie thought she could bear.

'I love Sky, Beauty, and I love your brother. I'm not interested in your opinion.'

Beauty recoiled and Bonnie knew her words had stung. But then Beauty straightened her shoulders as her eyes began to flash. 'I'm telling you Blaze just wants a mother for Sky. Are you really too blind to see that? Go ahead and think I'm making it up, but Blaze vowed he would find Sky another mother when Carrie and Prince abandoned her.'

Bonnie shook her head. 'What makes you feel you have to hurt everyone, Beauty? What is it?'

Beauty looked down and for a moment the fire died in her dark eyes. Then just as quickly it was back. 'What would you know of hurt, Bonnie Blake? I know, I know, you've had a few burns, but the pain passed. I've lived my whole life in pain.'

Bonnie said nothing, hoping Beauty would continue to open up. To her surprise, she did.

'You don't get it, do you, Bonnie? I killed my mother. Can you imagine living with that? Then I nearly killed you and Blaze and that little boy in the car. I'm a murderer and everyone knows it. I'm called Beauty when I'm ugliest one in my family. My father couldn't be bothered caring for me, and nobody has ever loved me. But I don't blame them. I don't like me, either.'

'Oh Beauty!' Bonnie gasped, hearing the anguish behind Beauty's anger. 'Blaze loves you! I love you!'

But although tears shone in Beauty's eyes, she had closed up again. She walked from the room and slammed the door.

Bonnie sat staring at that door for a very long time.

***

Beauty's bad mood continued well into the next day at school, and soon everyone learned that she and Nate had broken up. And so, fearing her spiteful tongue and fierce temper, they kept away. All except Chappy Eldwin. The class watched in anticipation as he approached her in his Charlie Chaplin walk; a sure sign he was about to entertain them all.

'Come on, Beauty,' He threw her a roguish smile. 'Dance with me.'

'Beauty is not my name.'

'It is according to your brother.'

'It's my circus name. Amy is the name on my birth certificate.'

'Amy. Hmm, sorry, but Beauty suits you better.'

She stepped toward him. 'Don't you dare call me Beauty again. Ever!'

Chappy ignored her fierce look. 'Okay, Princess Petunia.'

The class burst into laughter at the sight of him trying to reach for her waist and calling her by the name of a flower while her fierce look threatened murder.

'I don't know why you can't be serious!' Beauty raged at him. 'You act as though life is a joke. Well it's not!'

Chappy grinned at her anger and it infuriated her further. Without thought, she struck him across the face. She saw the split second of hurt that crossed his expression before he dramatically threw himself to the ground as though the slap had been too powerful for him, then turned a somersault and stood before her again, the grin still fixed on his face. The class shouted with laughter, while Beauty hurried away, horrified at what she had just done.

***

Chappy walked home that afternoon, deep in thought. What was it about Amy Clements that drew him to her? Why did he so badly want to see her happy? He touched his cheek where she had slapped him. The mark had faded slightly, but was still there. She was spiteful, and refused to make friends but something deep within drove him to persist. Maybe it was the flash of anguish he caught in her eyes every now and then. Or maybe it was the vulnerability she tried so hard to hide. And she had accused him of not being real!

'She's the one who won't be real!' He tried to be angry with her, but the reality was, she had come too close to the truth and it bothered him. The most spiteful, mixed up girl in the school had been the only one to see through him, to see that beneath his crazy, outgoing exterior he was afraid to be himself, afraid to admit that he also felt pain and he also feared rejection.

He lifted his eyes in prayer. 'Lord God, does it matter that I'm such an actor? You're my closest friend. You know who I am. Do they need to know?'

He loved to make people laugh. He felt as though he needed to make everyone happy. But why?

It was a question he would think and pray about until he found the answer.

Chapter Seventeen

Blaze poured himself into his work with the youth and his days were busy and full. There was no time for himself, but he didn't regret it. He saw the admiration in the eyes of the young people and felt it was all worth it. He loved the way he could encourage and reach them all with a word of advice, a helping hand, the gift of his time. In the pouring out of himself he was gaining so much and the guilt of past failures faded into the background.

'I have a new vision!' Blaze shared with Bonnie almost every day, his enthusiasm unquenchable, his drive unstoppable. He wondered at times why Bonnie would listen in silence. Once she had questioned where she fit into his ideas, but he didn't have an answer for her at the time.

It was Bible study night and Blaze had a message he knew these teens needed to hear.

'Without a purpose in life there is no hope, no direction.' He looked around the group, his eyes resting on the newest member. He had met Joey on the street one night and had been there for him ever since, supporting, encouraging and rescuing him from his old, destructive life. 'And our true purpose is the one God planned for us. Until we find what that is we can never be satisfied.'

Chappy nodded enthusiastically. 'That's why so many teenagers feel like they have no hope. Did you know they did a survey in our school and seventy-five percent of students have at least considered suicide within the last three years?'

Blaze gasped in disbelief, but Danielle backed Chappy up. 'It's true. They did the same survey at all the schools and the results were the same. It's hard to believe that life really is so empty for so many teenagers.'

Blaze was a study of concentration as he listened and his mind began to plan. 'They need to hear about Jesus. They need hope!' His eyes burned as he looked around the group. 'I wonder if I could get in to the schools.'

'Yeah, you'd be great!' Danielle moved closer and put a hand on his arm. Blaze glanced appreciatively in her direction.

'Why don't you try?' another youth suggested. One by one the youth began to encourage him in his new vision. Only Bonnie remained silent, watching as Blaze's eyes took on their familiar intensity. Then he began questioning the youth around him, finding out what they believed would reach their classmates.

***

The next morning a young man was pacing the office of the very school Blaze Clements envisioned reaching.

'You mean it's against the law to urge these teenagers to find purpose and hope in life?' he was demanding. 'It's against the law to save their lives?'

The answer from the principal was patient. 'No, Alex. It's against the law to present your beliefs as the only option. I know you have an amazing story to share and I have great respect for the way you were able to turn your life around and recover from a life of abuse, crime and alcoholism. You could be a great inspiration and role model for the students here, but legally I can't let you tell them God is the only answer to their problems.'

The two considered one another for a moment until Alex sat down. 'Okay, sir,' he relented, 'I will present my views as an option, as you put it, but may I have permission to share my life experience with them?'

'Of course.'

'Even if my life experience shows there is only one option, and that is to commit your life to God and find forgiveness and healing in Him?'

Slowly, the headmaster smiled. He was gaining more respect for this youth by the minute. For someone who claimed he had dropped out of school at the age of fourteen, he showed remarkable wisdom and intense determination.

'Are you sure you don't want to enrol in school again and complete your certificate?'

Alex shook his head, refusing to be put off. 'I just want to share my experience with these teenagers who are so much like I was, sir. Please give me that opportunity.'

The principal stood, holding out his hand for Alex to shake. 'You have my permission. Wednesday week we have our next Life Choice Seminar and we haven't organised anyone yet. Can you be ready by then?'

Alex's face broke into a beaming smile. 'I sure can. Thank you, sir!'

'Call me Geoff, Alex. Since you're not a student and don't plan to enrol, you may call me Geoff.'

'Thank you, Geoff.' He shook the principal's hand and left.

***

Blaze couldn't believe it. How could he have missed his opportunity? And only by a few minutes? Someone else had beat him to it. He had tried every tactic but was unable to convince the high school principal that his message for the students was of utmost importance and made it worth postponing classes.

'I don't think the Department of Education would be impressed if I didn't prepare these students academically because I feel their spiritual needs are greater,' Geoff explained to the persistent Blaze. 'One religious seminar a month is all the students need, and as I said, Alex is taking the next one.'

'It's not just a religious seminar,' Blaze insisted, wishing

Bonnie were not sitting in the room as he spoke on the phone. Her expression appeared too knowing. Why didn't she look surprised and sympathetic that he was unable to convince this man his message was important?

'I'm sorry, Mr Clements. We have already arranged all our seminars for this year. However, I can keep you in mind for next year.'

Blaze hung up and turned to Bonnie. 'I need to get in to that high school and give them a reason to live! I need to tell them about Jesus.' The deep furrow in his brow revealed his anguish.

'And they wouldn't let you?'

'They've got this other guy. He's high in demand in all the schools and they're not interested in anyone else.'

'Blaze,' Bonnie reached for him, drawing him to the lounge beside her, 'this other man might be reaching those teenagers in a way you could never imagine.'

'But I have such an important message to share!'

'And you don't think God can use someone else to give that message?'

Blaze's eyes turned from burdened to hurt and angry. 'You're not understanding what I'm saying. I thought you of all people would share my vision.'

Bonnie's look was sad. 'I do. I'm just saying God can use other people, too.'

Blaze did not find it easy to let go. He pressed on, trying to persuade the schools that he was the man they needed to speak to their students. It was urgent. In fact, a matter of life and death; eternal life or death. For that reason, he simply couldn't ignore the burden he felt for these young people. He tried every avenue he could think of, from conducting an art class, to beginning lunch time meetings to discuss issues concerning students. Each time, he found there was no place for him.

'I'm so tired of hearing the name Alex Goldsmith,' he finally admitted to Bonnie. 'Whatever ministry I try to get involved in, this guy has been there first and convinced them he's the one for the job. How on earth am I supposed to have an impact if I can't even speak to the students?'

'Blaze, are you forgetting that God's in control here?' Bonnie's question was gentle. 'He can get you in to the schools if He wants to.'

Blaze turned angry eyes to her. 'Are you saying God doesn't want me to share this message he's given me?' Before she could answer, he stood to leave the room. 'You're becoming way too patronising, Bonnie.'

***

He didn't see the look of hurt that passed over her face, but Beauty did.

'Why do you put up with that, Bonnie? He's so moody and he treats you like dirt. Why do you just take it?'

Bonnie shrugged. 'Because I love him.' She hesitated and her voice when it came out revealed her true hurt. 'And because he needs my support, not my criticism.'

Beauty shook her head in disgust. 'You're so blind, Bonnie Blake. I've told you; All Blaze really wants from you is a mother for Sky. He's so busy concentrating on being there for everyone else that he doesn't even know he's got a fiancée.'

Bonnie knew Beauty was right. Blaze didn't even seem to notice her any more.

***

Blaze was troubled. Was Bonnie right? Was he not trusting God? Was he trying to take on too much? He paced the house, coming to a stop in his art studio.

'Lord, show me please. What do you want me to do?'

He longed to paint again, but there was just no time for that kind of indulgence. Wistfully, he moved to his pile of canvases and his fingers itched to take up a paint brush. What would he paint? A vision of his father came to mind. A child in a man's body in so many ways. So jovial and upbeat. It made him a good circus employee, but not a good father. He tried to picture his father but his mind was racing so fast he couldn't settle on the form of his face.

'Go home.'

Blaze blinked. The sudden voice in his head was so clear. It came again. 'Blaze, you need to go to Everdeen.'

Blaze hadn't felt God's prompting for a long time now, but this was undeniable.

'Now?' he asked out loud, but he knew the answer. He needed to go and see his family. Was someone in trouble? He grabbed his wallet and keys and raced out to the car. Then he remembered Beauty and raced back in to scribble her a note saying he would be back later that evening.

He drove as fast as he could, continually pulling himself back to the speed limit. He couldn't explain to a police officer that he was on a mission from God if he was breaking the law, could he?

Blaze prayed the whole way, pouring his heart out to God in a way he hadn't for a long time. Yet God seemed silent.

'What do you want from me, God?' he pleaded. He was almost there. He sped up the dirt driveway. All was quiet. The horses were happily grazing in the paddock beside the house and nothing seemed out of place. He was about to step out of the car when he glanced in the rear-vision mirror. He stopped and looked again, then jumped out and spun around to look at the road outside their home. A magnificent horse stood in the middle of the road, not moving a muscle.

'Victorian Dream?' he called. What was his sister Misty's horse doing out there in such a dangerous place? A car could come around that corner at any moment.

To his surprise, the horse didn't respond to his voice. He strained his eyes and then he saw it. A crumpled figure on the ground beneath the horse. With a cry, Blaze ran out the gate.

'Misty!

She didn't move and Blaze rushed directly to her, his heart pounding in his chest. He crouched down and Victorian Dream stepped carefully to the side. Blaze wanted to hug the horse for saving Misty, but there was no time. He needed to find out if Misty was okay. He carried her carefully to the roadside, closely followed by Victorian Dream. He shook his sister gently, but urgently.

'Misty!'

To his relief, she was breathing steadily. But fast asleep. He had seen her fall asleep at the drop of a hat all her life, but never while riding a horse, and never in the middle of a road! After every circus performance she would collapse into an exhausted heap and sleep for hours. Something had to be bothering her terribly.

Carefully, he carried her inside the house. He studied her face, lined with strain, and the scar down her cheek. He remembered the day she got that scar. She had only been five years old and had fallen asleep after a performance. Once again his father had left him with the responsibility of looking after the younger ones while he took the horses back to their stalls. Together the children sat behind the big top curtain, waiting for him to return. Misty had climbed up onto one of the props used for the trapeze artists and closed her eyes. Then, without warning, she fell. Six year old Blaze had felt sick to the stomach when she let out a cry and stared up at him, blood streaming down her cheek. He was never sure what had cut her, but from then he watched her like a hawk after every performance, keeping her close by his side. She was his responsibility and he had let her and his father down.

Blaze's memories faded as Misty stirred. He hated to think what could have happened if he hadn't come home. The weight of responsibility felt too much, sometimes.

'Thanks God, for protecting her.' He frowned. But why had God brought him home to do it? Why couldn't his father have found her? Was rescuing people the gift God had given him? Bonnie needed to understand that God had given him this responsibility to care for others from when he was a small boy. It wasn't his choice; it was his duty.

Misty stirred again, then opened her eyes, blinking several times.

'Blaze?' She breathed in a deep sigh of relief. 'You're home!' Blaze nodded as she stared around the room in confusion. 'What happened?'

'You fell asleep in the middle of the road, Misty.'

She sat up. 'I what? On the road?'

Blaze nodded again and watched as tears filled his sister's dark eyes. 'Why do I do that?' she almost pleaded. 'After every performance I just need to sleep. Now we don't perform any more, but it still happens.'

Blaze gathered her in his arms while she continued to cry. 'Lord, you know life is hard for Misty. Please help her through. Give her strength. Take whatever it is that makes her so tired, and give her the answers she needs. Thank you for keeping her safe today. You still perform miracles and we can be in no doubt that you love us. Help us live for you and leave our lives in your hands.'

Blaze talked more with his sister and made sure she was okay before heading home again. He knew his job was done. Lately he had felt restless and dissatisfied despite all the people he had helped, but today he felt at peace. Why? It was a question he tried to answer all the way home.

Chapter Eighteen

Bonnie walked toward Blaze's home, deep in thought. She loved Blaze, but it seemed he had forgotten she even existed. Now that his concern for Sky was no longer foremost in his mind he didn't seem to need her at all. It was true he should first be committed to God and that she should support him in that role, but was Blaze really doing what God was asking of him or was he trying to make up for Derek's death? There had been such a change in him since Derek's funeral. On the surface, his passion for God's work appeared right and good but something was missing. Bonnie couldn't help suspecting Blaze wasn't really ministering out of love. He was ministering out of a feeling of obligation. Out of guilt.

Bonnie shook her head sadly. Blaze had once looked upon her with such deep love. But now, the only time his dark eyes held any kind of passion, they were filled with anguish or anger. Yes, Blaze's anger and guilt was consuming him.

'What can I do, Lord?' she prayed. 'What would you have me do? Please direct and guide me.'

Bonnie thought of their wedding, only two months away. Her mother had been busily planning and the youth group were excited and asking to be involved. Only Blaze seemed disinterested. Only he seemed to forget he had once ached to spend every moment with her.

She was relieved when he answered the door. At least he had remembered. Or had he? He had the car keys in his hand.

'Hi, Bonnie. I'm just off to Reece's. He needs to see me. Says he has an urgent decision to make.'

Bonnie's brows raised. 'What about Bible study preparation?'

'Don't worry about it. I'll do it later tonight.'

'But Blaze, you've prepared and led every Bible study on your own for the last month.'

Bonnie's exasperation was beginning to show, and Blaze put a gentle hand on her shoulder. 'I know, but that's okay. This is important. Reece is choosing his subjects for next semester. It could change the direction of his life and he has to decide by tomorrow. He desperately wants to do God's will.'

Bonnie tried to hide her disappointment, but she was feeling near breaking point. 'I thought we decided it was best to lead Bible study together, then break off into groups.'

'Yeah we did, but it just doesn't seem to be working out that way.'

Bonnie bit her lip to keep from saying what she was thinking. It would have worked if Blaze could find a few moments to spend with his fiancée instead of acting the hero and answering every cry for help.

She tried again. 'Remember you offered to cook me tea after Bible study preparation?'

Blaze grimaced. 'Oh, sorry about that. I've had a huge day. Another night perhaps?'

Bonnie's voice held a gentle reprimand. 'Blaze, I don't think you've kept an appointment with me for a long time now. I think I need to find your diary and put my name down in there somewhere. Then you won't be able to forget.'

'I don't usually forget. Things just come up,' Blaze shuffled restlessly, looking to his shoes at the front door.

'Have you forgotten it's your day off?' Bonnie tried one last ploy.

'You're being selfish, Bonnie.' Blaze no longer hid his irritation. 'Reece needs me right now and people's needs don't always arise on the days I'm working.'

'What about Mr Mathison?' Bonnie insisted, hurt that he considered her selfish. 'Why couldn't he help?'

Blaze shook his head. 'Reece asked me, Bonnie. Not Mr Mathison.'

Bonnie fell silent, hating the tension she felt between them. He gave her a quick hug. 'How about we meet at my place tomorrow morning? We'll talk about it all then.'

'I have lectures at uni in the morning.'

'The afternoon then.'

Bonnie had little choice but to agree as she left the house. There was no reason to stay any longer.

***

Blaze watched Bonnie go, then rushed to put on his shoes, jumping when the phone rang.

'What now?' He hated to keep Reece waiting, but he grabbed the phone.

'Blaze, please come round here! Quick!' Danielle's voice was breathless and pleading.

'Danielle? Are you alright?'

'I'm not sure. I'm here on my own and there's these drunk guys walking along our street. They're smashing bottles and stuff.'

'Where are your parents?

'On their way home from Melbourne. Dad had to see a specialist about his broken leg. They'll be a few hours.'

Now Blaze was concerned. 'Have you called the police?'

'No. They haven't done anything wrong but I'm scared.'

Hearing the noise of glass breaking, and recognising the genuine fear in Danielle's voice, Blaze reached for the car keys.

'Hang on Danielle, I'll be right there.'

By the time he arrived, the men had gone, but Danielle was still visibly shaken. 'Can you stay with me?'

Blaze looked into her wide, fear filled eyes and agreed, so long as he could phone Reece and speak with him. Rather than the long discussion he had planned to have with Reece, Blaze had to be content with speaking with him over the phone for twenty minutes

112

with a frightened Danielle sitting close by his side. By the time he headed home his heart was heavy, his mind and body weary. If only ministry were easier!

***

Bonnie sensed how weary Blaze was the moment she walked into his lounge room the following afternoon. He lay back on the lounge, long legs stretched in front of him, eyes almost closed. Had his meeting with Reece really taken that much out of him?

'Is everything okay with Reece?'

She saw Blaze's shoulders stiffen and wished she hadn't asked the question. Still, she wanted to be involved in Blaze's ministry, even if it did steal her own time with him.

'It went well.'

'He's chosen his subjects?' Bonnie pressed.

'I think so.'

'You didn't help him fill in the form?'

'No, we just talked about it.' Blaze was being evasive so Bonnie decided to change the subject.

'What did you think of his new car?'

Blaze hesitated, then slowly turned to her. 'I didn't see it. I didn't get to his house. We just talked on the phone.'

Her surprise was evident in her eyes. 'Why?'

'Danielle had an emergency. There were some drunks heading down her street and her parents were away. She was scared.'

'So you went there on your own?'

Blaze nodded and Bonnie frowned. 'Why didn't you pick me up on the way?'

'I … she needed me there straight away. I didn't know if those guys would be bashing her door in.'

'Couldn't you have called me to come once you got there and saw she was okay?'

Blaze's expression was apologetic. 'I didn't think of it. I rang Reece straight away.'

'But what about the policy we have?' Bonnie felt betrayed. 'What if people saw your car there and made assumptions?'

Blaze gave a guilty look and avoided her eyes. 'If people want to start rumours they will, but I'm more concerned about the safety of those I'm responsible for.'

'You don't care about your reputation?'

'Of course I care about my reputation!' Blaze slammed his hand down on the coffee table, causing Bonnie to jump in fright. He stood and paced. 'In ministry I have to care about my reputation, but the wellbeing of those I love is way more important!'

'Those you love?' Bonnie whispered, shock showing in her wide blue eyes.

'Oh come on, Bonnie!' Blaze lowered himself down and sank as far back into the lounge as he could. 'You are deliberately taking everything I say the wrong way. I care about every member of our group. Yes, I love them. All equally. All deeply!'

Bonnie continued to stare at the angry young man before her. The only time she saw the deep intensity of feeling in Blaze's eyes was when he was angry. It used to be love.

'Don't punish me with silence.' Blaze's voice was quieter, but his body was taut with restrained anger and frustration.

Bonnie felt her throat begin to ache as she held back tears. She wasn't trying to punish him, she just didn't know what else to say. Everything hurt. He was sounding more like Beauty every day and she couldn't deal with it. Not now. She stood. 'This anger is consuming you, Blaze. I don't want to talk when you're like this. Call me when you've calmed down.'

She moved to the door, trying to contain her tears until she was safely away from him. But in a flash, Blaze was standing before her.

'Please don't leave.' His expression softened when he saw her tears. 'I'm sorry I got angry. I just feel so alone in my ministry sometimes.'

'Oh Blaze,' Bonnie moaned. 'I feel so alone, too. Can't we work together?'

'Let's try,' he agreed, but he sounded defeated. Bonnie allowed him to lead her back to his lounge room. She sat beside him, preparing to share her ideas for Bible study. Before she could speak, he pulled out some notes.

'This is how I thought we should do it.'

Bonnie listened in silence. He didn't seem to want her contribution, so she didn't offer it. When he had finally planned the whole thing, she stood to leave, allowing him to give her another quick hug. She had done little, but she arrived home exhausted.

'Bonnie, you're home!' Her mother sat at the table busily sorting through names of wedding guests.

Bonnie pulled out a chair and glanced through the guest list. Mrs Blake sighed. 'We still have too many and I just don't know who to cut out. I wish we could afford them all, but…' She shrugged, and Bonnie sat up straighter.

'It would be so much easier on you not to have to do all this, wouldn't it?'

Mrs Blake smiled and reached a hand to her daughter's shoulder. 'It's a lot of work,' she admitted, 'but knowing you will be marrying Blaze after all this time makes it worth it.'

Bonnie fell silent as she watched her mother return to her work. She glanced at the piles of invitations of the table. 'I wonder what happens when people cancel their wedding at the last minute.' She fiddled with a piece of coloured ribbon, unable to look at her mother. 'I mean, what happens to all the invitations, the decorations, the dress?'

'I guess they can sell the dress.' Her mother looked up and her expression changed. 'Bonnie?'

Bonnie gave a sad smile and shrugged, but her mother was looking at her intently.

'What's happened? Do you wish you could cancel?'

Bonnie met her mother's eyes for a moment, and then glanced away. 'Maybe.'

Immediately, her mother came to her. 'Bonnie, what is going on?'

It was clear her mother was trying to remain calm despite the shock of the revelation and Bonnie felt tears welling in her eyes. 'I don't know. Things just aren't right. Blaze is so busy all the time and he only has time for other people. Things are really tense and he thinks I'm selfish for not understanding why he has no time for me. He's different now, and I worry that even once we're married it won't change. I've tried talking to him about it but he just gets really angry.'

Mrs Blake sat back down and absently ran a hand down the guest list. 'I have to admit I've noticed he doesn't drop by anymore. And you've started sitting with us at church. I should have wondered about that.'

Bonnie nodded. It was always her making the effort to visit or call Blaze. And at church Blaze spent all his time with the young people, hardly even acknowledging her.

Mrs Blake bit her lip. 'Funny how I thought nothing of it until now.'

'Mum, what should I do?' Bonnie's lip quivered as she fought tears. 'Everyone is so happy for us, and the wedding is nearly all finalised. You've done so much.'

Mrs Blake took Bonnie by the shoulders and spoke urgently. 'Bonnie, you do what you know is right. Forget the cost, the work, everything. The wedding is just a day. The marriage needs to be something you can live with for a lifetime.'

Bonnie shook her head in defeat. 'But how do I know what is right? How do I know what God wants? I don't want to do something I will regret for the rest of my life.'

'Then ask God to show you.' Her mother stood and drew her daughter into her arms, holding her tight. 'He will show you. And you'll never regret it.'

Chapter Nineteen

It didn't take long for people to realise that Nate and Beauty were enemies again. The romance which had been the talk of the school, now became everybody's favourite conflict. All the school students waited to see who was going to take the next action in the ongoing battle.

First, Beauty found vegemite spread through her locker. She responded by wiping the substance on Nate's Biology work book. His reaction was to tear up her Geography notes and leave them strewn across the oval. With glee, Beauty then wrote his name across a desk in black texta and waited with anticipation to hear his name on the detention list for defacing school property. Sure enough, it came.

'But I didn't graffiti anything!' she heard Nate complain to the teacher on duty.

'Then how did your name get on the desk?'

'Someone else must have put it there. It's not even my writing!'

Beauty poked her head through the door. 'Just do your detention, Nate!'

'Get out, Miss Clements,' the head teacher called back, 'or you can join him.'

Casting Nate a triumphant grin, Beauty disappeared, but not before she saw understanding dawn on Nate. She waited for his next move with both dread and anticipation. It didn't take long for him to track her down.

'Think you're smart, don't you?' He stood before her as she sat by her locker, reading the novel Bonnie had loaned her.

'Don't you?' Nate repeated when she ignored him. Still, she continued reading. Suddenly Nate grabbed the book from her fingers and Beauty jumped up to retrieve it.

'Give it back!' He was holding the book above the bin.

'Don't even think about it. It's not mine.'

A slow smile spread over Nate's face. 'Even better. Explain this to the owner.'

Before she could stop him, he took the drink bottle from beside her and poured it over the book.

'You idiot!' she hissed, striking out at him. He fell back from the force of her blow, while she rushed to his locker and took the first book she could find. Angrily, she began tearing it up, page by page until it lay in pieces before him.

'You are the idiot.' He held his hand to his now swollen cheek. 'That's a library book.'

Beauty glanced around. An interested crowd had gathered to watch the scene, so there was no way she could deny who had destroyed the book. And there amongst the onlookers was the head teacher. His eyes bored through both of them. 'You two come with me. Now.'

'I hate that life isn't fair,' Beauty complained to Blaze as she explained how she had just received two days' suspension. 'I can't stand feeling helpless and not in control.'

'Why is that?'

Blaze's gentle tolerance annoyed her. She wished he'd get angry with her and be over with it. He had that look on his face – the one that said he was ready to fix all her problems when he had no idea.

'Is it because you feel your life is out of control?' he pressed. 'Because you can't accept God is in control and knows best?'

'Stop preaching at me.' She flung the principal's note into Blaze's hand. 'I am just sick of people, full stop.'

Blaze turned the note over and began to read before he looked back to her. 'Why are you determined to be so difficult? Do you take pleasure in making people dislike you?'

She continued to glare at him, but he appeared unfazed by her eyes shooting daggers at him. He came closer but wisely didn't touch her. 'I know what it is, Beauty, even if you don't. You're so afraid of rejection you won't even give people a chance to love you.'

She opened her mouth to retort, but he held up a hand and continued.

'I think that if you can blame yourself for being hated, if you can be in control of why people reject you, you feel safer. There's nothing worse than being disliked for who you really are. So you won't let anybody close enough to see who you really are.'

Beauty frowned, not liking the way Blaze came so close to the truth. She put on her best sneer. 'All that psycho mumbo jumbo. Do you even know what you're talking about?'

'I'm talking about what's in your heart.'

'What? Anger?'

'No, beneath that.'

'There's nothing.'

He shook his head. 'At Bible college, we learned that anger is a secondary emotion. Another emotion is always there, being masked by the anger.'

Beauty turned from him. 'You're doing it again. Don't try your psychology on me. The last thing I want is my religious brother trying to work out how my mind works.'

With that, she went into her room and closed the door. Blaze would forget about her soon enough. Bonnie was coming that afternoon to choose songs for the wedding and for the first time in a long time Blaze had remembered.

***

The moment Bonnie arrived, Blaze began telling her his concerns about Beauty. 'I just don't know how to deal with her sometimes.' A deep frown creased his forehead. 'Perhaps we should put our

119

wedding off until things are sorted out. But that would mean making Sky wait even longer for a real mother.'

Bonnie's face paled. She had asked God to guide her. She had asked for an indication she should cancel the wedding. Now Blaze himself had suggested they should put it off. And not for their sake, but for the sake of his sister and niece. Once she had admired his love and concern for others. Now she resented it. She couldn't marry a man whose ministry she resented.

'Then again, I'm sure it'll be fine,' Blaze was saying. 'I think Beauty just needs more time and attention. She needs to understand our wedding won't change my love and concern for her.'

Suddenly he stopped short as though truly seeing Bonnie for the first time. 'Bonnie? Are you okay?'

She swallowed hard. 'I can't marry you, Blaze,' her voice came out in a hoarse whisper. 'I don't know how to be a mother.'

Blaze's expression was one of shock and hurt. 'What's this got to do with being a mother?'

'Don't get angry,' Bonnie pleaded, turning away. 'This is hard enough already.'

Blaze wrung his hands and paced. Finally he sat down and looked directly into her eyes. 'I'm sorry. Please explain what's going on.'

Bonnie hesitated, then looked directly at him. 'I just … I want you to love me as I am. Not as a mother for Sky and sister for Beauty. Not as someone to encourage you in whatever vision for ministry you have at the time.'

Blaze's eyes darkened again. 'What did Beauty say to you?'

She shook her head. 'Blaze, this isn't about Beauty. This is about you and me. You are too involved in being a father to Sky, Beauty and the rest of the youth group to have a wife.'

Blaze looked surprised. 'Isn't that what a wife is for? To be part of the family?'

'Yes, but the husband and wife relationship needs to come first. You only need me because Sky needs me and because the youth group wants me. It used to be more than that, but it's not anymore.' Bonnie felt emotional pain she had never felt before as she looked into Blaze's eyes which no longer held the depth or intensity they once had when he looked at her. 'You only look at hurting teenagers the way you used to look at me.'

Blaze sighed and drew her to him. 'Bonnie, ministry costs.' He sounded wistful. 'I didn't think it would cost this much, but it does. I do still love you. Everyone knows that.'

'Do they? Even Beauty sees the difference, Blaze.'

'She told you that and you believed her? You know she's angry and mixed up. She's tried to hurt us from the moment she arrived.'

Bonnie shook her head, hating the anger that had returned to his tone. 'She was right, Blaze. I have known it for a while but didn't want to admit it.'

Finally, Blaze's look was defeated. 'What do you want me to do? What is it you want from me?'

Bonnie had no response. She couldn't demand love. She couldn't demand his attention. It was a choice he would have to make on his own.

Chapter Twenty

It was hard turning up for youth group, knowing the news would soon be public knowledge. Bonnie tried to give her usual cheerful smile, but failed miserably.

'What's wrong, Bonnie?' Danielle's eyes were full of curiosity as the teenagers settled into Blaze's lounge room. 'Have you and Blaze had a fight?'

Bonnie shook her head, trying to hide her finger now empty of an engagement ring. Danielle never missed a thing. And as the study began, Bonnie knew Danielle's keen eyes were taking in the way she and Blaze avoided each other's eyes despite leading the study as a team. She was taking in the way they were almost too polite to one another. And then, when Bonnie stood to collect a Bible from the shelf, Danielle moved in next to Blaze, sitting as close to him as possible and throwing him a charming smile.

'I reread the book of Mark three times this week,' she told him. 'After your last week's study, I just had to read it over and over. You're a gifted Bible study leader, Blaze.'

Blaze smiled back at her, but his response was vague. There was distinct sadness in his eyes. Bonnie knew she had done that to him. Had she done the right thing?

'So how's wedding preparations coming along?' Danielle asked pointedly when it came time for prayer. 'I see you've lost your engagement ring already, Bonnie. Not a good start.'

There was an awkward silence before Blaze cleared his throat.

'Um, well, actually, we have called off the wedding.'

Bonnie swallowed the sob trying to rise up in her throat as the members of the youth group looked from Blaze to her in disbelief. All except Danielle, whose look was knowing.

'What happened?' the teenagers wanted to know.

Blaze looked to Bonnie and she knew it was her responsibility to answer. She had thought this through carefully. 'We have our own personal issues we need to sort out before we can commit to something like marriage.'

No one questioned that, but the mood after that was subdued, though everyone tried to carry on as normal. During supper, Bonnie watched Blaze laughing and talking with the members of the group and tried to grasp reality. She still loved him so much, but he wasn't her fiancé any more. She knew she had done the right thing, but how it hurt! Silently, she slipped out onto the back step and looked out into the starlit night.

'I still love him, Lord!' God seemed so far away right now, but she had to believe he was there. She needed someone to take her aching loneliness and assure her everything would be all right. 'Oh God, be my refuge,' she wept, 'and shield me from this pain. It hurts so much!'

Finally she managed to pull herself together and head back inside.

'I think we still work well as a team,' Blaze told Bonnie as the teenagers filed out the door and Bonnie picked up her own Bible and notebook, preparing to leave. 'I don't want the youth group to lose you because of what has happened between us.'

Bonnie studied him thoughtfully, trying to ignore the way her throat ached with the tears she had just spent as she poured her heart out to God on Blaze's back step.

'Will you still work with me?' Blaze pressed. His dark eyes gazed into hers. 'I truly believe we'll get this thing sorted out, Bonnie. I'm not giving up.'

Bonnie nodded, her heart leaping with hope. Perhaps one day, Blaze would have time for her again. Maybe things would change, after all.

Those hopes were dashed only a few days later. She had just seated herself in Blaze's lounge room ready to prepare their next week's study. As usual, they had gone through their formal greetings and Blaze had looked anywhere in the room but at her. Beauty came to join them and began a carefree conversation about her schoolwork.

'School seems so easy for some people,' she told them. 'Like Chappy Eldwin. He's always mucking around instead of working, but he seems to pass every subject easily.'

'I remember someone else who was like that,' Blaze commented with a grin, looking directly at Bonnie for the first time since she arrived. Bonnie played with the bracelet on her wrist, trying not to smile.

Beauty looked surprised. 'I thought you were a good student.'

Bonnie's lips twitched. 'I was.'

'Not good,' Blaze corrected. 'Proficient but very distracting.'

'Ooh, big word!' Beauty was laughing, but Blaze was glancing at his watch. Then he jumped up. 'I have to go.'

'Go where?'

'Danielle has asked me to her pool party.'

Bonnie couldn't believe it. 'But Blaze, we arranged to go over next week's Bible study. That's why I'm here.'

As soon as she said the words she wished she had just let it go.

'Oh, that's right.' Blaze looked sheepish for a moment, then shrugged. 'I forgot. We can do it tomorrow, though.' At Bonnie's look, he stopped. 'Or would you prefer to do it now?'

It was clear Bonnie was still not his priority and the reality hit hard. Biting words began to flow from her mouth.

'No thanks. You go and flirt with Danielle. I'm okay left here by myself. I've survived every other time, haven't I?'

Blaze flinched and remorse hit Bonnie as hard as the hurt had.

'What would you care?' Blaze demanded.

Bonnie's eyes widened in disbelief. And to think she had just felt sorry for her sarcastic comments. He had no idea!

'What would I care?' She lifted her hands in question. 'That's right. What would I care that you are planning to marry me one week and flirting with someone else the next?'

Confusion covered Blaze's face. 'You broke it off. You were the one who fell out of love.'

'I never said I don't love you!' Bonnie cried in exasperation.

'Then what did you say?'

Bonnie shook her head and left without another word.

***

Blaze saw nothing else to do but go. He was about to grab his wallet when he saw Beauty's face. Her expression was one of pure disgust. He stopped to face her. 'What now?'

'You don't even know? You're pathetic, Blaze.'

'Me? I'm pathetic? Beauty, you are the one who told her I don't love her any more. You are the one who convinced her to break it off with me, so don't start.'

'I'm sorry, big brother, but I didn't have to convince her. You did that very well on your own.'

Blaze grabbed his wallet and shoved it in his back pocket. 'Well if caring for other people is an unforgivable sin, then go ahead and condemn me.'

He watched as Beauty grabbed the car keys from the hook on the wall and threw them into his chest. 'Then go and do your caring! But if you have any sense in your head you will go and care for Bonnie, not Danielle!'

Blaze tried to put Bonnie and Beauty from his mind as he drove to Danielle's home, but somehow the sunny afternoon seemed clouded.

'I'm living with a thunderstorm!' he thought as he pictured Beauty's face, 'and Bonnie isn't much different these days.'

He hadn't even reached the front door before Danielle was at his side.

'Blaze, where have you been? I thought you mustn't be coming Come on, everyone's already out the back.'

125

Blaze tried not to notice her brief bikini as he followed her out to the pool. Before he knew what was happening, Danielle had playfully grabbed the towel from his shoulders and pushed him into the pool. Those around laughed with delight as their youth leader came up spluttering, looking around for Danielle. She stood on the edge, smiling a seductive smile.

'You disappoint me, Blaze,' she said, when he just looked at her. 'I would have thought you'd have sought revenge by now.'

'Revenge is mine, says the Lord.' Blaze quoted from the book of Romans, trying to avert his eyes.

Danielle's eyes were sparkling with laughter and teasing. 'Then be his instrument!' Blaze shook his head and turned away. For the first time he realised his caring may just have given Danielle the wrong impression. Was this what Bonnie had seen? Did she think he shared Danielle's feelings?

Danielle's attention seeking from that moment was so direct it was tiring. How was he supposed to love her and let her know he wasn't romantically interested at the same time? There was a lot to be said for the wisdom of allowing Bonnie to reach out to the girls.

He didn't stay long. He returned home feeling empty, but burdened. It had suddenly become clear to him that Danielle might truly think he had feelings for her. If he didn't, she was determined to do her best to encourage them. Seeing the light flashing on his answering machine, he went over to play the messages.

'Blaze, this is Bonnie,' her clear voice said. 'I'm so sorry for what I said and how I said it. Please forgive me. I love –' She stopped short, about to finish in her normal way. 'Um, Goodbye. See you soon.'

Blaze shook his head, anguish filling him. 'Lord, what can I do?'

And then he knew the answer. Pray. It felt so unfamiliar to cry out to God for help. He hadn't done it in a long, long time. In fact, he had been working on his own for months now.

'I'm sorry, Lord. Help me include you.' He turned to go to bed. It had been a long day. A long week. In fact, a long, hard, year.

CHAPTER TWENTY ONE

Chappy had seen Blaze leave the pool party in a hurry and was troubled by the haunted look in his youth minister's eyes. He needed to talk to Danielle about her behaviour. He might end up hurt himself, but someone needed to talk to her.

'Danielle, can I see you for a minute?'

Danielle glanced up from the group of girls she was now standing with. 'Can't it wait?'

Chappy considered. 'No, not really.'

Danielle frowned in annoyance. 'I'm sure it can. Go clown around for a while.'

She was cut off as Chappy grabbed her arm and pulled her away from her group of friends. Danielle's look was one of hurt and surprise, but his anger kept him going.

'What's wrong with you, Danielle? What did you think you were doing with Blaze? He's only just broken up with his fiancée! You could have given him some space.'

'Jealous?'

Her smile was patronising and Chappy wanted to shake her. A muscle jumped in his jaw. 'No. I just don't want you hurting Blaze or Bonnie. He needs time.'

'Why?'

'Because love is not a tap you just turn on and off. It goes deeper than emotion.'

Danielle turned on him with a sneering expression. 'Oh, and

you'd know, Chappy Eldwin! After all, it's much more than emotion that draws you to the pretty Amy Clements, isn't it?'

Chappy stared at her, lost for words for a moment. Embarrassed that Danielle recognised his feelings for Beauty, he looked down. 'Yes, it is,' he responded quietly. 'A lot more than emotion.'

Danielle shook her head in disgust. 'You're fickle, Chappy.' Her voice dripped with venom. 'You rely on being a comedian for your popularity, but only because you have to. There's not much more to you.'

With that, she turned her back and returned to her friends.

Chappy tried to forget Danielle's words, but they bothered him. Did he really feel attracted to Amy Clements because of her appearance? Surely it went deeper than that? As he came to Blaze's door a few days later, his Charlie Chaplin walk in play, he prayed for strength. Another Bible study and another chance to see Amy, or Beauty, or whatever her real name was.

'Help me keep my focus, Lord. She's not even a believer … yet.' He smiled, knowing God promised to answer prayer, and praying for Amy Clements was something he had been doing persistently from the day he met her.

'Please help Bonnie and Blaze sort things out,' he prayed next. He ached at Bonnie Blake's sorrow. On the surface she smiled and laughed as usual, but he could see the pain beneath her exterior happiness.

'She's like me,' he admitted to himself. 'Pretending everything is great and life is fun but hiding deep pain underneath.'

***

Bonnie glanced up as Chappy Eldwin entered the room. As expected, he moved toward the chair she was in, ready to dive amongst the pile of bodies. But this time only Bonnie lay there and she was stretched from end to end, leaving no room for anybody else. Chappy's eyebrows raised in surprise. He glanced to the other teenagers who were looking at one another, not sure whether to comment or let it be.

Bonnie watched the way Chappy gave an amused shake of his head and moved to another chair, his eyes never leaving hers. What are you up to? his eyes seemed to ask, but he didn't speak the words.

Blaze came out from the kitchen, paused mid-step. 'What's everyone standing around for?' Then he saw Bonnie and began to smile. 'Push her off.'

Bonnie planted herself more firmly in place.

'You push her off,' Chappy retorted, his eyes twinkling a challenge.

Bonnie began to flip nonchalantly through a magazine as though totally unaware of the discussion going on around her.

'I think you're asking for trouble, Bonnie Blake,' Blaze said, still smiling. Bonnie felt her throat constrict at the sound of that deep, familiar tone. How she missed him!

'I disagree,' she responded simply, still flicking casually through the magazine and believing she had won. In the past, Blaze may have sat on her or pulled her off the chair, but he respected her decision to break off the engagement and had avoided any physical contact with her since. Besides, Bonnie really hadn't expected Blaze to become involved. It had been a spur of the moment decision to take the most popular lounge chair before the teenagers arrived. She hadn't really known how they would react, but certainly hadn't expected them to just stand and look at her the way they did. Maybe she truly was too old to tease and joke around like the teenagers did with one another. She wasn't going to back down now, though. She was too curious.

Blaze took a step toward her, and for a moment she wondered if he was thinking about tackling her to the floor. Then he turned abruptly and headed for the kitchen. Moments later, he returned and Bonnie screamed as he poured a glass of water over her.

'Bonnie's wet herself!' Danielle laughed, while Bonnie looked at Blaze in amazement. Once over the shock, she jumped up from the lounge, dripping water all over the floor. Then she rushed at him. His eyes widened in surprise at her reaction, but just in time he escaped the room and raced out the front door, closely followed by Bonnie and the rest of the group. Then began a water fight unlike they'd ever had before. Everyone was out for themselves and no one was left dry. Bonnie didn't think she had laughed so much in a long time. A little more tension dissolved with each bucket of water thrown.

'Okay, time to finish and get some Bible study done,' Blaze finally instructed the group. Bonnie was exhausted from chasing and being chased. She was also drenched. She glanced up at Blaze and saw that his eyes were on her. They were warm and open and she took in a sharp intake of breath. He hadn't looked at her that way in a long time. She was reminded of the reason she first fell in love with him, but the moment was broken as Danielle smiled up at him. 'You still have a dry spot on your shirt, Blaze. Look.'

She ran her hand over it, drawing everyone's attention to the form of his muscles beneath his shirt. Bonnie was aware Danielle had been by Blaze's side most of the evening and he had spent a large proportion of the time defending himself from her one-sided attacks. The off-handed way he now glanced at Danielle and returned his gaze to Bonnie spoke volumes.

With what seemed like a great effort, he tore his gaze away. 'Come on everyone, let's head inside.' He ushered the teenagers toward the house and Bonnie watched. She had never actually managed to get him wet, despite that intent being the whole reason the water fight began. It reminded her of the incident when she was a teenager – she had tried to cover Blaze in horse manure but somehow he had managed to escape. She had been so bold back then – so carefree and haphazard. Some of that old mischief rose up within her and she crept up to the tap. Blaze was behind the group obediently heading into the house and if she was quick enough she could get him before he was indoors.

The water pouring from the tap into the saucepan was loud in the absence of shouting, screaming teenagers and Blaze turned back to see what Bonnie was doing. His eyebrows raised as recognition filled his eyes.

'Don't you dare,' he warned, but that only hastened Bonnie's progress. Her heart began to beat faster as he strode toward her, his eyes alight with laughter. Before she knew what had happened, he had rushed at her and grabbed her arms, forcing her to drop the saucepan. It clattered to the ground at her feet. She struggled against him with everything she had, but he managed to force her around until she found herself pinned against him.

She gasped and froze as she dealt with the emotions rushing through her at his closeness. Biting her lip, she tipped her head back and looked up at him. He caught her eye and gently released her. She read the silent apology in his expression and tried to turn away before he read too much of the feelings in her own eyes. She knew she was too late. There was no doubt Blaze saw into her eyes and her heart that she still loved him, but mixed with that love was deep hurt. A shadow passed over his face as he looked up to the watching teenagers.

'Come on, let's find some towels and then get the study done.'

His voice came out abrupt and Bonnie wanted to cry. Ministry cost so much.

***

Witnessing the encounter through her bedroom window, Beauty shook her head. She hated what she was seeing, what she had done. Why had she wanted to hurt Blaze and Bonnie? It was true their happiness had heightened her own loneliness, but nothing could be worse than seeing their pain – the pain she had once thought she wanted. She needed an escape.

For the first time since breaking up with Nate, she headed to the local night club. It was quite easy to slip out of the house. She knew it would be hours before the distracted Blaze would look into her room and realise that once more she had disappeared without telling him where she was going.

The music was lively and soon Beauty was caught up in the atmosphere, dancing her way through the crowds. It no longer mattered that Nate had broken up with her. With each drink, it began to matter less that Blaze and Bonnie had lost their happiness.

Chappy heard the quiet close of the front door and looked up just in time to see Beauty escape out onto the street and disappear into the night. He was afraid for her. If she was going where he thought she was going, tonight was the worst night. He had heard stories about the people at the local nightclub on Wednesday nights.

'Lord, what should I do?' He glanced at Blaze, who was clearly oblivious to his sister leaving as he led the group through their Bible study. Bonnie looked as though she were lost in a world of her own. He couldn't just let Beauty go. Anything could happen. But if he left now he would be questioned. He would just have to wait until the study was finished and leave before supper.

It was almost an hour later when Chappy crept into the night club, scanning the room for any sign of Beauty.

'Have you seen Amy Clements?' he asked several people. Most of them shrugged or ignored him, too drunk or drugged to comprehend his question or remember who they had seen that evening. Chappy searched each room, looking for any girl with long, mahogany coloured hair and praying for her safety. He moved quickly, desperate to find her before she was introduced to the heavy drug scene or something worse. He almost ran past the scantily dressed women who eyed him suggestively. He had to find her. Now.

'Lord, help me!'

Then he saw her. She was hunched on the floor by the billiard table. The room was empty tonight – the people who frequented the club on Wednesday nights were interested in far more sinister pursuits than a game of pool.

'Amy.' Chappy raced to her side and knelt down. 'What are you doing?'

It was obvious she was drunk again and sadness filled Chappy. Not for Blaze's sake, but for hers.

'Yell at me, Chappy,' she slurred as she raised bloodshot eyes to look up at him. 'Tell me you hate me.'

'Hate you? I don't hate you.'

'Well, you should!'

Chappy shook his head, wishing he could understand this girl.

'Go on,' she insisted. 'I hit you, remember.' She raised tear-filled eyes to his, then reached a trembling hand to his cheek, to the spot her slap had left fiery red. 'And I'm a murderer. I destroy all happiness.'

Chappy sat down beside her and she lay her head on his shoulder. Surprised, he studied her more closely and saw by her red-rimmed eyes that she had been crying for quite a while.

'That's not true.'

'It is. I killed my mother and Monty and a little boy. I nearly killed Blaze and Bonnie and now I've ruined their relationship.'

Chappy took her hand, wondering just how many secrets Amy Clements held in her troubled heart and mind. Normally he wouldn't take advantage of her openness when she was drunk, but tonight he just had to know. 'What do you mean you killed your mother?'

Her open, honest answered surprised him. She told him everything, from her mother dying giving birth, to asking Bonnie to rescue a horse from burning stables, Blaze getting tetanus, the accident with her horse and the car and, finally the way she caused Bonnie to believe Blaze didn't love her anymore. She poured out her whole story while Chappy listened in stunned silence.

'I deserve to die,' Beauty concluded, tearfully.

'You do,' Chappy agreed, and her head jerked up as she stared at him in shock. 'We all do, but someone has already died on our behalf. You don't need to feel guilt anymore.'

'What do you mean?' She shook her head and rubbed her eyes, straining to see him better through her blurred vision. 'Please tell me. I need to know.'

He shook his head. 'I'm not going to explain tonight. You're too drunk to remember what I say, anyway. I'll come and see if you still want to know tomorrow.'

He rose to his feet, then reached a hand to help her up. Once again, it would be a long walk home, but he would make good use of the time, begging God to reach in and reveal himself to this hurting, drunk teenager.

***

When Beauty awoke in the morning, things were different. For the first time, she remembered every detail of her drinking binge the night before. She remembered Chappy's concerned kindness and his words that were a lifeline. She had told him everything but he hadn't seemed shocked. Instead, he told her she need not feel guilt – there was hope! Despite that hope, her face flamed with shame at the memory that he had seen her so drunk again. Or was she really drunk? The drinks had had a different effect on her last night. At first there was the glorious oblivion to all worries, but then came another dimension. A deep, confusing sorrow. How many times had Chappy seen her that way? she wondered. She dragged herself out of bed, knowing she just had to get to school to see Chappy.

'You're grounded.' Blaze's voice grated on her as she came into the kitchen. She would have come back with a retort but she saw the anguish in his eyes. Instead, she surprised him with an apology.

'I'm sorry. I won't do it again.'

Blaze was dumbstruck. Clearly he had been expecting an argument about why he should have any authority over her. Confusion filled his eyes as he turned from her and Beauty wished she had the courage to give him a hug. If only life could be a little easier for him; for her. Everything was becoming too much to bear.

'Chappy!' Beauty called as she saw him walking through the school gate with his friends. He turned from them to approach her.

'Amy,' he returned, searching her face as though trying to find something deeper in her tired, dark eyes.

'You said you would talk to me today.'

He nodded, and his eyes lit up. 'You remembered!' The school bell went, signalling time for class and he sighed. 'How about after school?'

Beauty nodded. She was grounded, but nothing could be more important than this.

'Come and meet me at the town hall.'

She nodded again, determined to be there. She knew the town hall he spoke of; a large, brick building a few doors down from the school.

However, through the day, her courage began to fail. Could she really defy Blaze again? And what would Chappy say to her? Perhaps she was just setting herself up for more hurt. Perhaps her hopes would be totally dashed. Yet somehow she believed the meeting would change her life. For that reason alone, she wondered if she really would gather up enough courage to go. Change could be frightening.

The long school day was finally over. Tentatively, Beauty crept into the town hall, wondering what would happen this afternoon. What she saw as she entered amazed her. The hall had transformed into a ballroom. Dancers moved around the floor with their partners, but there in the middle of them, the clumsy, comic Chappy was leading a young woman around the floor with graceful style. His every move reminded her of smooth, flowing water.

The instructor stepped into the middle of the floor as the music stopped. 'Okay, that will do for today.'

Chappy released his partner and turned to catch sight of Beauty. He flashed her a smile and came to her, taking her arm. 'Come on, let's go.' He grabbed his school bag and led her out the door. Beauty thought she understood his rush to get away. He didn't want to be seen to be an item with her.

She turned to face him, hands on hips. 'You never told me you can really dance.'

He pulled her along, down the footpath. 'It's part of my Higher School Certificate. They gave it as an option instead of music.'

'But you're really good at it. You deliberately make everyone at school think you're clumsy.'

'Hmm.' He gave her a cheeky smile, while she tried to slow down.

He was urging her on despite her resistance and she attempted a glare at him. 'What's the rush?'

'I presume you're grounded again and I don't want you in more trouble. So I figure we need to talk as I walk you home.'

Beauty frowned. 'What makes you think I'm grounded?'

He grinned. 'You deserve to be.'

She pulled a face, but her eyes lit up with keen interest. 'So talk.'

His gaze became serious. 'Okay. I said I would share something with you that will take away your guilt.' She nodded. 'It's simple, really.'

She looked up the road to where her house was. 'It needs to be. I'm nearly home.'

He chuckled. 'Ah, so you are grounded.'

She screwed her nose up at him.

'It's like this,' his expression became earnest. 'I'm just as bad as you; I have as many reasons to live in guilt as you do, but I came to a point in my life where I asked God to take that guilt. You've heard about the cross?'

She nodded. Blaze had told her many times how Jesus had died on her behalf. She had also seen Blaze's powerful paintings, but she had never quite understood what it all meant.

'All you have to do is ask Jesus to forgive you and exchange his perfect life record for your imperfect one. Everything that's held against you will then be held against Jesus instead.'

Beauty frowned. 'That hardly seems fair.'

Chappy nodded. 'I know, but that's true love. The work is already done. Jesus already died on our behalf, so why waste it? Besides, we are giving him something in return. All he wants is our friendship – for us to become his adopted children. It's amazing, really. That same God I have hurt is my best friend. I talk to him more than I talk to any human. And the good thing about him is he knows my hurts, my joys … he knows my heart like nobody else does.'

'Your hurts? You act like you don't have any.'

'I know. But I do. Everyone does. Only I have someone to turn to. I don't carry around that awful feeling of guilt anymore, because he took it from me once I was willing to let it go and hand it all over to him.'

Beauty gazed at him, her eyes desperate and dark with emotion. She grasped his arm. 'Chappy, I'm sick of living with this guilt.'

'Then you need to give it to my friend, Jesus, and make him your friend, too.'

Beauty looked down, daring to hope this moment would change her life for the better. 'Show me how and I will.'

Chappy's smile lit up his face. 'So you want to confess your sin to God and let Jesus' perfect life record replace yours?'

She nodded, and there standing on the footpath, he led her in a prayer of confession and commitment to God.

'I've really messed up, God,' she admitted brokenly copying Chappy's words. 'And I need your help. I know I don't deserve your help, but I know you died when I am the one who deserves to. You paid for all my mistakes so please overlook them all. I want Jesus to take my messed up life record and give me his perfect one instead. Please be my friend and help me stop messing up so bad!'

'I've never really had friends before,' Beauty admitted to Chappy with a shy smile as she finished her prayer. 'I'm not really that nice a person. Are you sure God wants me?'

Chappy grinned. 'I'm sure. He made me want you as a friend, anyway.'

Beauty stared, then tears came to her usually angry, defiant eyes. Chappy put his arm around her and she struggled with emotion. Her challenging, arrogant expression disintegrated and her whole face lit up with the smile that came through her tears.

'So, all sorted?' Chappy asked, returning to his usual, lighthearted tone.

Beauty drew in a deep breath, her eyes shining. 'More than you could know.'

His eyes closed for a moment as he drew her into another hug. 'You know, I really had no idea leading someone to God could be sc simple or so dramatic and incredibly uplifting.'

'Dramatic.' Beauty grinned. 'Yeah, that's me. So dramatic.'

He became serious again. 'I've heard that it can be dramatic – the change God makes in a person. But most of the time it's a gradual, slow process. You ready for it?'

She nodded. 'Definitely. I wish it happened years ago!'

'So next time that guilt overwhelms you, remember it's not yours anymore, because you have a God who loves you and gave his life to take it away.'

Beauty grinned at him. 'Got it. No need to preach at me. I get enough of that from Blaze.'

He studied her a moment, then grinned cheekily. 'Right, and we all know how well that worked. I'll try something else. Do hugs work better?'

Beauty stepped back with a laugh, unwilling to admit that perhaps they did.

Chapter Twenty Two

Blaze was typing up the Bible study he was preparing for next week. He heard Beauty enter the house but couldn't bring himself to stop mid-thought.

'Blaze, can I talk to you?'

He kept typing. 'What's up?'

When she said nothing, he stopped his typing and looked at her. Her expression told him she had something important to say and wouldn't begin until she had his full attention.

'What's up?' he asked again.

'Nothing's up. I don't even need your counselling. I just wanted to tell you something.'

He shrugged. 'Go ahead.'

She swallowed hard. 'I'm a Christian now.'

'Pardon?'

'I'm forgiven! Guilt free. I've been thinking about it for a while. Chappy and I talked about it on the way home and I made the decision. I've given my life to God.'

Blaze was speechless. How could it be? He had been so concerned about how little time he had spent with Beauty and now, now she had become a Christian anyway. Somehow the news bothered him as much as it thrilled him. It seemed Bonnie's words were true. God could and would work without him, even to bring his own impossible sister to believe.

Beauty left before Blaze could respond and slowly he stood and turned off his computer. He needed some fresh air. A long walk would do him good.

His thoughts went to the day he had told Bonnie of Beauty's accident. He remembered how they had prayed together that she would come to know and love God. At the time, he had known he alone could not have an impact on his sister's life. Despite knowing that, he had begun to plan exactly how he would go about having an impact. There were so many things he could do, so many things he could say, and yet none of them had worked.

'Only God can change lives,' he reminded himself softly. 'Only he knows our hearts.'

He wondered where along the line he had forgotten that. He thought of Bonnie. Gentle, wise, understanding Bonnie. Hadn't she tried to tell him? Quickly, he put her out of his mind as he turned and headed back home. The thought of her brought too much pain.

***

Seeing that Blaze had left, Beauty crept into his studio, longing once more to see the picture of her family and the cross overshadowing the word 'guilt'. It had been so long since she saw it, yet its profound message was now so clear and personal to her. Many nights as a child she had lain awake, imagining her mother's still, lifeless form, and taken the guilt and pain upon herself. Now it was gone. She was set free.

As she searched through each canvas, she stared in awe at the images before her, marvelling at her brother's gift. She paused as she came across a picture which took her breath away. There, gazing up from the canvas was a life-like picture of Bonnie Blake. Stepping back with a gasp, Beauty let the canvas fall back into place. She couldn't bear to look at that picture, for Bonnie didn't look that way any longer. Those lively blue eyes now gleamed with sorrow. The sparkle of life had gone. Beauty felt the sting of tears as she turned and headed to the door. She stopped short as she came across Blaze standing in the doorway.

Blaze arrived home to hear the noise of the canvases falling back into place and went to investigate. He stared in surprise when he saw Beauty there. She had always insisted his art was of no interest to her, but there she stood with tears welling in her eyes, the first tears he had seen since the day his honesty had hurt her so deeply and the bright little eight year old had run from him.

'Beauty, what's wrong?' Compassion took over and he ached to see her tears.

'I'm so sorry,' she said, swiping at them.

'For what?'

'For making life so hard for you.' She ran into his arms and, stunned, he held her as she sobbed her heart out. His throat tightened and he swallowed hard against the lump forming there.

'I love you, Blaze.'

Blaze drew in a deep breath, then tried to respond but his voice broke. 'I love you too,' he finally managed. Then the two stood that way for several minutes, Blaze's heart in turmoil. He knew healing was happening in his sister's life, so why was his own heart still in anguish?

She stepped back and looked into his eyes. 'Blaze, why don't you paint anymore?'

Blaze subconsciously frowned. 'Painting was just a phase I went through, a phase that had no results. I need to be there for people, not paint for them.'

'But your painting had an impact on me.'

Blaze shook his head, 'And on Derek,' His tone was dry. 'I was so bound up in the things I enjoyed doing rather than being there for people, and that killed him.'

Beauty grasped his arms. 'Stop it, Blaze! You're doing just what I did for so many years!'

'What do you mean?'

'You're placing guilt on yourself for something that you can't change. Jesus dealt with it when he died on the cross, but if you keep holding onto it, it will weigh you down until you break. I know because I've been broken for years. Don't do it to yourself!'

Blaze frowned, planning his defense but she cut him off.

'You don't need to explain to me. I've been there, in that prison I made for myself. I'm asking you to accept God's forgiveness and get on with life. Don't try to pay for what Jesus already paid for on the cross. I'm asking you because I love you.'

Blaze was stunned into silence as his sister swept from the room. Could this really be Beauty, the sister who so often told him not to preach at her? Her words began to eat into his heart.

***

'I've been thinking about you and Bonnie,' Beauty told him as they washed up together a few days later, 'and I think I know what's going on between you and God and you and Bonnie.'

Blaze gave a bemused smile as he filled the sink with washing up water. 'Okay, enough of the pay-back, Beauty. I know I used to preach at you and I'm sorry. But you don't know all about me, okay?'

Beauty shook her head, 'No, just hear me out on this one. Please?'

Blaze shrugged and turned his back as he piled plates in the sink. 'Okay, I'm listening.'

Beauty came to stand beside him so she could see his face. 'Well, it's like the preacher was saying at Chappy's church this morning. You think you can buy God's love by doing things for him when he already loves you and just wants to spend time with you. Time is what counts.'

'Is that right?' Blaze looked sad. 'And I suppose you think I've been trying to buy Bonnie's love, too?'

'Well, I don't know, but I know she just wants to spend time with you. Why don't you –'

'Beauty, can't you see, it's too late?' Blaze cut her off. 'I've made a mess of things with Bonnie. I messed up, okay?'

Beauty nodded. 'Exactly. But now you can be forgiven.'

142

Blaze shook his head in frustration. 'Yes, but forgiveness doesn't mean I get away with it without any consequences. Being a Christian for a few days doesn't make you an expert on my life, Beauty Clements!'

'No, but being guilty for a lifetime does.'

'No, it does not! Doesn't it count that I've been a Christian for years and that I've counselled many more Christians than you've ever talked to!'

'There you go, acting as though you're better than me again.' Beauty sounded unusually subdued. 'Remember, you're just forgiven. That's all. And so am I.'

Blaze stared, wondering at her calm tone. It bothered him that she wasn't as worked up as he was.

'Remember ages back when you asked me what was in my heart beneath the anger? Well, I found out. It was guilt.'

'Okay, I'm glad you found out!' he said sincerely, 'but don't try to transfer your findings onto me. Now let's get this washing up done.' He focused on the plate he was washing.

'Don't you want to know what I was guilty of?'

She clearly wasn't going to let this go. Blaze let his shoulders slump. Having a sister who had her own personal relationship with God was a lot harder than he had expected. He let out a deep sigh. 'Okay, tell me.'

'Manslaughter.'

That had his attention. Was she having a go at him? She knew he had been accused of manslaughter when Derek took his life. His heart began to beat hard. This was too much to deal with right now. 'I'm glad you realised you're not guilty and sorted it out.' He was sincere, but dismissive. She wouldn't let it go.

'No, Blaze, I was guilty. I am. But God took it. Maybe I didn't really kill Mum, but I certainly played a part in the death of that little boy.'

Blaze dropped the dish he was holding, his look incredulous. 'You thought you killed Mum?'

'Indirectly, yes. She died and I have life.'

'But that's ludicrous!' He was pacing, now, his eyes wild. She was calm.

'Just like it's ludicrous – or whatever that word is – to think you killed Derek. Mum chose to have me. I had no say in it. I wasn't asked. The fact that she died doesn't mean it's wrong for me to enjoy life and be happy. Derek chose to drive that car into a pole. You had no say in it. You weren't asked.'

Blaze sat down again, his eyes darting around the room, searching for something, anything to hold on to. To get his bearings. Something inside his chest physically hurt and it was getting worse.

'But he needed me.'

'He needed God. You're not God.'

Suddenly Blaze could bear it no more. Great sobs wrenched from somewhere deep inside and tore out through his heart and into the air. He bent over in agony, his shoulders shaking. He missed Bonnie, he missed the peace and joy he had once felt. He missed the freedom of helping people for the pure joy of it. He lived out his punishment every day, in every phone call he felt obligated to answer, in every cry for help he had to respond to … in every moment he spent away from Bonnie, his closest friend.

An arm came around him and he was aware of Beauty there beside him. Her tears were dripping down onto his shoulders. 'Blaze,' she whispered, 'Let it go. Please. It's destroying you!'

And in that moment he lifted his eyes and cried out, 'God, help me!' Then he reached for his sister and they clung to one another.

A knock came at the door, causing Blaze to jump. If only he could have a few minutes to pull himself together he might be okay, but there wasn't time. If only he could leave the door, but it was as though he were dragged toward it, afraid it might be a life-threatening emergency; that someone needed rescuing again. If it was Danielle he would have to send her to see Bonnie. He moved toward the door, aware that Beauty had slipped away into her room as she usually did whenever someone came.

To his surprise, the church minister stood outside with Bonnie's father. He drew in a deep breath, hoping they wouldn't be able to tell he had been so emotional only a few minutes earlier.

'Mr Mathison, Mr Blake, come in.' He opened the door with a forced smile. The men smiled back but both looked serious as they seated themselves on his lounge. Blaze's heart beat hard in his chest. Was everything alright with Bonnie? If anything ever happened to her …

Mr Mathison leaned forward and his look made Blaze uncomfortable. 'Blaze, I owe you an apology.'

Blaze frowned in confusion, but the minister continued. 'I should have been around here a long time ago, praying with you, guiding you, supporting you.'

'But you have been. We meet once a week to pray for the youth and you go over all my study notes.'

Mr Mathison held up a hand. 'Yes, yes, we do. But who prays for you? Who gives you the support you need? Even ministers need to be held accountable, to be supported, loved and encouraged. You seemed so mature and coped so well with the whole Derek incident that I forgot you are still young in your faith, and that you don't really have anyone to come alongside you, especially now that Bonnie is no longer your fiancée.'

Blaze swallowed the lump that had returned to his throat. The compassion he saw in the eyes of the men before him was nearly his undoing.

Mr Blake now leaned forward. 'I owe you an apology, too. Rather than come and ask what was going on with you and Bonnie I just felt angry. I didn't think about what you're going through, what you might need. Bonnie has two supportive, loving parents. You've never had that. I wanted to provide that role, but the minute you hurt Bonnie I turned my back on you.'

Blaze stood up. He couldn't stand sitting there with these two men looking at him with such caring concern. He drew in a deep breath, took a step forward then a step back. How could he escape?

'Blaze, look at me.' Mr Mathison's voice was a gentle command.

Blaze forced himself to stop and look.

'Just consider what I have to say for a minute, will you?'

Blaze nodded and forced himself to sit down.

'What if all the work you have been doing for the youth is not what God has asked of you?'

Blaze's eyes widened. Was he about to be sacked? Did they not think he was a good enough youth minister? What had he done to deserve this? Hadn't he given everything for this ministry? He stood again, but Mr Mathison came and laid a firm hand on his shoulder, stopping him from pacing.

'Blaze, what if you threw away the responsibility God gave you to love and care for Bonnie for some sacrificial ideal you made for yourself after Derek died? I don't believe God ever asked you to give up Bonnie for ministry. I think maybe you've thrown God's gift back in his face. Taking on things he never asked you to do is just as bad as not doing what he asks of you.'

Blaze's hands came up to cover his eyes. He bit his lip, willing the pain in his chest to go away so he could think straight.

'But I do believe God has asked this of me. He confirmed it. I felt God tell me to go home and it saved my sister's life. It was so strong I could almost hear the voice out loud. If it wasn't God, then who?'

His eyes pleaded with the two men.

'It may well have been God,' Mr Mathison agreed. 'But what about all you're doing for Reece? What about Danielle? All the young people? Do you hear that same distinct calling from God or do you feel obligated to help them? Has all the time you spent with them saved their lives or has it helped them depend on you instead of God?'

Blaze heard Mr Blake stand too, and then felt another hand on his shoulder. Had God sent these men? Did God care that he was at breaking point and want to show him a way out? He opened his eyes and faced them.

'I don't think I know how to stop,' he admitted, biting his lip. 'I don't know how to let go. I made such a mistake with Derek. I'm so scared it will happen again.'

Both Mr Mathison and Mr Blake shook their heads at once and Mr Mathison squeezed his shoulder.

'Not a mistake, Blaze. You made a wise decision and I wish I'd made that so much clearer to you at the time.' Mr Mathison sighed. 'Derek made his own choice. Even Jesus let people choose to turn away. What about the rich man, Judas, the Pharisees?'

'So what do I do now?' Blaze's voice trembled. 'What am I supposed to do?'

'Have some time off. You've worked on all your days off for a long time, now. I want you to take a week. Go to the church Chappy Eldwin goes to and take your little sister along, too. Forget all responsibility and spend some time crying out to God, asking him what he wants from you. I think you'll find it's a lot less than you've been giving, but a whole lot more, too.'

Mr Mathison and Mr Blake prayed with him, and Blaze watched them leave, hardly knowing what to think. Despite his confusion a small ray of hope and peace was finding its way back into his heart and he grasped it with both hands. 'Lord, help me find my way back to you!'

Chapter Twenty Three

Beauty loved going to Chappy Eldwin's church with Blaze by her side. He seemed a lot more relaxed and she enjoyed talking with him about her new-found faith. She also enjoyed the contemporary songs and messages she heard at church. Blaze admitted it was a lot more laid back than the church he ministered in and that he enjoyed it, too. However, she saw the sadness in his eyes and knew that he missed Bonnie. Without Bible study or church, there was no excuse to see her anymore.

Beauty knew things had changed for Blaze. He was still sad, but there was a thoughtfulness in his eyes that hadn't been there for a long time. He began ignoring the phone and spending more time poring over his Bible. Often she would find him sitting quietly, his eyes closed, and she knew he was praying. She prayed, too.

The more she saw the sadness in Blaze's eyes, the more she thought of Bonnie. She couldn't get her from her mind.

When Blaze left the house to meet with Mr Mathison and Mr Blake for a prayer time, Beauty made her way directly to the portrait of Bonnie. She stared at it a few moments. It was so clever, so lifelike. It was world class. With that thought, Beauty rushed to the phone.

'Chappy, can you come over? I want to show you something.'

She paced for the few minutes it took him to get there. 'What took you so long?'

'Come on, I came as fast as I could!' he defended himself with a chuckle. 'I even knocked over my dad on the way out and broke his leg, but to save time, I told him to crawl to the phone and call the ambulance himself.'

She chuckled at him and pulled him inside. 'Quick, I need to show you something before Blaze gets home.'

He gave her an amused look but went along with her. 'Okay, quick, let's go.'

She grabbed his hand and dragged him to the back room, then paused and looked at him earnestly. 'You know how Blaze and Bonnie broke up?'

'Yeah.'

'Well, he still loves her. Look at this!' She moved the canvases until she came to the one of Bonnie. A Bonnie with joy and peace radiating from her wide blue eyes, yet covered in burn scars just the same. 'Beauty' the title beneath was displayed.

Chappy gasped just as Beauty had done. 'It's brilliant!'

They both gazed at it in silence for a few minutes. Finally, Chappy pulled it out from amongst the other canvases. 'What a pity it's hidden.'

'Just like their love for each other, isn't it?' Beauty agreed. 'Hidden when it deserves to be displayed. There's no way Bonnie could doubt Blaze's love if she saw this.'

Chappy turned from the painting to stare at her, then frowned. 'You have a plan?'

Beauty shook her head. 'No, you're supposed to come up with a brilliant plan. That's why I called you.'

He frowned harder, then began to smile. 'Amy, I do believe I have an idea!'

Beauty chuckled at his tone, a light in her eyes. 'Tell me!'

'Well,' he rubbed his chin thoughtfully, 'There is another art competition at the art gallery this week. We should enter this! And when it wins, perhaps it will just remind those two clowns that they really do love each other. It might get Blaze painting again, too.'

'But what about Bonnie? She needs to see this herself.'

'She does, and she needs to see Blaze, too. We need to get them to that art gallery at the same time; make them run into each other.'

Beauty bit her lip. 'But how do we get them both to the gallery at the same time?'

'Easy. You ask Blaze to spend some time with you. Tell him you need to talk about a few things. And ask him to take you to the art gallery. He'd never turn you down. You know how he is when someone needs to talk.'

'Yeah, anyone but Bonnie. It's like he thinks it's sin to do anything he enjoys, and because he loves Bonnie, he thinks he has to sacrifice that or it's not ministry.'

'Warped, isn't it?' Chappy shook his head sadly. 'I hope you are aware that our whole plan might not work.'

Beauty was incredulous. 'Why wouldn't it? Surely he will change when he realises he still loves her?'

'It's very hard to change a habit, especially when it's linked to so many deep hurts.' Chappy gave her a meaningful look. 'Believe me, I know all about it.'

'You do?' Beauty's dark eyes scrutinised him and he turned away for a moment. She watched the way he forced himself to turn back.

'I'm talking about my clowning around.' He swallowed hard. 'I started clowning when I was about eight. My brother got a brain tumor and I thought that keeping him happy might just help him get well.'

'And it didn't?' Beauty had never seen Chappy so serious.

'No. The sicker he got, the more I clowned around, but toward the end he was too unwell to laugh anymore and then too sick to even recognise me. We had some special times together though and I loved to make him laugh. It was such a change from seeing his frightened look. I think I made him forget his pain for a bit.'

'And you've just never stopped clowning.' Beauty wished she could somehow take some of the pain from Chappy.

'I think I still clown for him,' Chappy's eyes focussed on something far in the distance. 'It keeps him alive, somehow.'

Suddenly he looked at her again. 'And when I clowned for you, I wanted to take the pain from you, but I had to realise that I can't do that. Taking people's pain is a miracle only God can perform, the one he performed on the cross when he took our sin on himself. I can change the expression on their face and make them laugh, but I can't heal their hearts.'

'I know. That's what Blaze needs to understand,' Beauty said, moved by Chappy's revelation.

'Yes, but only God can show him.'

'So are we trying to do God's job by entering this painting?'

Chappy studied her seriously for a moment. 'You might have a point. But then again, maybe God has prompted us to do this because he wants to use it.'

'So what do we do?'

The two studied one another for a few moments before Chappy bowed his head. 'Lord, guide us in this. If we shouldn't enter the painting, then don't let it be accepted into the competition.'

It was surprisingly easy to enter the painting. Mr Eldwin was delighted to accept an entry from the previous winner. To their relief it didn't seem to occur to him to question why Blaze would get his sister to enter the painting for him rather than doing it himself.

'He's amazing, that youth leader of yours,' Mr Eldwin said to the pair as they handed over the painting. Chappy nodded. 'He's not without his faults, though, Dad.'

Mr Eldwin raised his eyebrows in surprise. 'You've had nothing but praise for him in the past, Chappy. What's happened?'

Chappy merely shrugged, and Beauty smiled knowingly. 'None of us are perfect, are we, Mr Eldwin?'

Mr Eldwin smiled. 'No, I guess not.'

***

The opening of the gallery for public viewing came only a few days later. Beauty awoke from her sleep, bright with anticipation. 'Please God, let it work.'

Blaze had been distant and quiet these last few days. He hadn't mentioned Bonnie once and Beauty began to have her doubts.

Perhaps Chappy was right. Some habits were too hard to change. Perhaps Blaze's love for Bonnie really had died. But then a vision of Bonnie's face and the painting came to mind. Beauty knew it couldn't be true. Love like that couldn't just dissolve. Ever.

***

Bonnie was only too pleased to be looking through the art gallery with Chappy. She had been lonely lately and Chappy was entertaining company. She missed the times she had spent looking through galleries with Blaze in the past. Through Blaze's gift with art, her own interest had grown. Chappy knew something about art, although not as much as Blaze. Frowning, Bonnie now tried to put Blaze from her mind. Often she wondered if the wound of losing him would ever heal.

'It just takes time,' her mother had assured her and Bonnie wished she was right, while knowing nothing in the world would ever take the feelings she still held for Blaze Clements.

They headed toward the judge's table, and Mr Eldwin jumped up and rushed to her with a beaming smile. 'Chappy, you've brought the object of the winner's affection.' He held out a hand to Bonnie. 'And Blaze is right, isn't he, son? She really is the picture of true beauty.'

'Pardon?' Confusion filled Bonnie but Mr Eldwin was chuckling.

'Blaze didn't tell you he was entering your picture?' Before she knew what was happening, Mr Eldwin took her by the arm and led her to a side section of the gallery. His hand swept up to the painting with a large first prize ribbon slung across it.

Bonnie gasped. It was her. She couldn't help noticing the peace and joy that shone from the eyes looking back at her. Her burn scars were there, but this particular young woman was indeed beautiful. She shone with life and joy. Pain struck her chest. Was this how Blaze still saw her? He did love her once.

But what on earth had made him enter this picture in the competition? They weren't engaged any longer. Clearly Mr Eldwin didn't realise that. He was still talking on and on about the joy of

152

true love, while Chappy looked uncomfortable and tried to stop his father's flow of words.

'Are you and Blaze together again?'

Bonnie turned at the familiar voice. Oh no, Danielle was there and had seen the picture, too. This time Bonnie had no answer. Were they? Was Blaze trying to tell her something by entering this picture? She moved away, needing space. Danielle was the last person she wanted to see right now. In fact, she wished she could be alone, but the art gallery was so full of people. She had nowhere to go, nowhere to turn.

***

As Blaze entered the gallery, he noticed a well-dressed young man gazing at him with admiration. The stranger was smiling as though something significant was happening. Puzzled, Blaze turned away. He hadn't ever seen the man before.

'Here is Blaze Clements himself!' one of the official looking women standing by the door announced, while all those standing around began to clap and cheer.

Puzzled, Blaze leaned down to whisper in Beauty's ear. 'What's going on?'

Beauty gave him a beaming smile, her eyes filled with excitement. 'I entered one of your pictures and you won! Oh Blaze, you won! Again.'

'What picture?' Blaze demanded, trying to smile at the cheering people and hide his confusion.

Beauty grabbed his hand. 'I'll show you. You'll never believe it. This is perfect.' She led him toward the open theme section.

The moment Blaze saw the picture he also saw Bonnie standing to the side, her gaze fixed on it. He saw the hurt and confusion in Bonnie's wide, blue eyes and shook his head as he turned on his sister.

'What did you think you were doing? What an insensitive thing to do!'

His voice had come out louder than he intended and Beauty's

153

smile instantly faded and turned to horror. Blaze followed her gaze and saw the look of anguish passing over Bonnie's features before she slipped away through the crowd. The familiar pain began to beat a tattoo in his chest and he tried to race after her. He had to explain, let her know he didn't enter that picture. He wouldn't do such an inappropriate, insensitive thing. Yes, he would have liked to, but as their relationship stood right now, he knew he had no right.

He reached the door, wildly looking around for Bonnie, frustrated by the person who stepped in his path.

'Blaze, can I speak with you?' Distractedly, Blaze met the gaze of the well-dressed stranger he had noticed earlier. His face still held that wide-eyed admiration. Blaze didn't know what to do. He wanted to make the right choice. Bonnie or this young man? Who needed him most? No, who did God want him to talk to right now? He glanced toward the door again. Bonnie had gone. He so badly wanted to follow his heart; to follow her, but …

'Blaze, you don't know me,' the stranger was tentative, almost nervous. Blaze gave him a friendly, though still distracted look, inviting him to go on. The stranger shuffled a bit, then took a deep breath. 'Blaze, I'm the one who destroyed your painting.'

He had his attention now. Blaze glanced toward the painting which was still intact.

'Not this one.' The young man's voice now held a tremour. 'The one of the sheep.'

Blaze couldn't speak. What was he talking about? He opened his mouth, but the man was continuing.

'I was so angry with that councillor making money for abused children when he had no idea what abuse is all about. I began destroying paintings, but yours … yours had an impact on me. For the first time I understood and believed in God's love for me. I found my purpose in life.'

'You became a Christian? Through my painting?'

'Yes. I couldn't get that image out of my head. I knew I needed to be loved like that, so I went in search of God, the only one who can love so deeply, so sacrificially. I've always regretted destroying that picture, but I know God has forgiven me. Can you?'

Blaze pulled himself together as his mind worked through all he had just been told. Bonnie had always told him that picture would change lives although so few saw it, and here was evidence it had changed at least one. Bonnie was so right, so wise.

'I can't draw,' the young man said, 'but I have told so many people about that painting which changed my life and people have turned to God through it. I prayed and prayed that some day I would meet the man who painted it. I came here first thing this morning to see if you had entered another of your masterpieces. Praise God you did!'

Blaze smiled and then stopped as he saw the name on the young man's badge. Alex Goldsmith.

'You're the young man who has made such an impact on the high schools,' Blaze realised, while Alex shook his head.

'Not me. God. But he's used your painting in ways you probably could never have imagined possible. Blaze, please paint that picture again. If you've forgotten any part of that image, I never have and never will. I can't paint, but I can tell you what to paint. I'd love to have it with me as I go around the schools. The real picture truly paints a thousand of my words.'

Blaze looked down, emotion overwhelming him for a moment. 'Our God is good,' he finally managed to whisper.

'He is,' Alex agreed.

Blaze grasped the young man's arm. 'I've made many mistakes, Alex. I must also ask your forgiveness. So many times I was angry that you were able to have ministry in the schools while I couldn't.'

Alex's eyes widened. 'You were? I'm sorry, I had no idea. Of course you're forgiven.'

'Thank you. I will paint that picture again. But please pray for me right now, because there's someone else I have to go and see to ask forgiveness.'

Alex nodded and watched as Blaze rushed after Bonnie.

Blaze's heart and mind were overwhelmingly full as he rushed after her. Bonnie had been right. He had forgotten God was in control and had tried to reach everyone on his own.

'Lord, help me find her. Please. Give me the words. Please give her back to me to love, to cherish, to give my heart to.'

He glanced around the street. There was a park across the road. Then he saw her. She sat, a lone figure on a park bench, her head in her hands. He instinctively knew she was crying; that her heart was in as much pain as his. In that moment, he knew that many times he had caused this incredible woman to cry. He raced over, praying that God would make something good come from the horrible mess he had made.

****

Bonnie felt his presence before she saw him. He stood looking down at her, his dark eyes filled with a shadow of pain and regret. 'Bonnie, I'm so sorry.'

His deep voice came out broken and she brushed away her tears. 'It's okay. I'm okay.'

He gave a tired sounding chuckle and lowered himself to the seat beside her. 'You're not okay. You've tried that line on me before.'

When she didn't respond, he took her hand, causing her to draw in her breath. His eyes gazed into hers. 'That painting upset you, didn't it?'

The caring in his intense, dark eyes only deepened the pain she was feeling. So long ago he had always looked at her like that.

'I just dared to hope.' She gave a helpless shrug.

'That I entered it?' When she gave no response, he moved closer and put an arm around her shoulder, gently moving the hair from her face. When she froze, he looked down at her hand and ran his finger along the scars the way he had so long ago. Surprised, Bonnie looked up at him.

'Blaze, we're not ...'

She couldn't finish, for Blaze pulled her closer and tenderly touched his lips to hers. Unwilling to pull away, both just stared at one another until Blaze spoke, his voice coming out in a whisper.

'I've missed you so badly, my Bonnie. Please forgive me for my selfishness and foolishness.'

'Blaze, we both –'

'Please let me finish,' he pleaded, and she fell silent.

'I've been bound up in guilt, Bonnie. I tried to make up for what happened to Derek by making sure it couldn't ever happen again. I forgot that God's in control, and most of all, I became too afraid to love. I thought I didn't deserve the precious gift God gave me in you, but once I lost you, my life felt empty. It hurt so badly. It still does.' He touched a hand to his heart. 'It's like a physical pain, right here, and it won't go away.'

Bonnie stared at him, speechless, while he knelt down on one knee. He took her hand, and gazed up at her, his eyes imploring her to read into his heart.

'Will you marry me, Bonnie? Will you take me back?' There was a distinct tremor in his voice. His old confidence was gone, but his eyes spoke of a deeper love than could be put in words. 'I love you. I always have.' Tears forced their way from beneath his eyelids and down his strong jawline. 'I know I don't deserve to have you back, but will you … can you have me?'

Bonnie cried too hard to speak, but her answer was obvious when she threw herself into his arms and clung to him. They held one another, both crying out their pain and at the same time rejoicing that this time they truly would become husband and wife. When Blaze released her his eyes were filled with an overwhelming tenderness.

'I can't wait to walk through this life with you, Blaze.' She reached her scarred hand out to him with confidence. 'We'll help each other walk with God, accept his forgiveness and reach out to others.'

'Thank you.' His voice became hoarse and he gave her a shy smile. 'Am I allowed to kiss you?'

She gave the hint of a smile. 'I thought you just did.'

'Again?' His mouth twitched and she smiled as she lifted her face to his.

'Yes. And how about every day for the rest of our lives?'

Blaze didn't need any further invitation.

Chapter Twenty Four

Bonnie sat in her nursing lecture trying to concentrate, but her thoughts kept returning to Blaze. He had promised things would be different. He assured her God had touched and changed him, but how could she be sure? With all her heart she longed to believe him, but there were still doubts.

She sighed restlessly, thinking of the painting Chappy and Beauty had entered on Blaze's behalf.

'It worked! It worked!' Beauty had laughed in joy when she was informed of the renewed engagement. Chappy had just grinned as though his mouth would split.

'I prayed and prayed it would work!' Beauty laughed, while Bonnie stared in amazement. Beauty praying?

'It's okay, you can close your mouth,' Beauty grinned at her. 'I'm forgiven now.'

'Forgiven?'

'Yes, I believe. I'm a Christian, as you put it. I've given my life to God.'

Bonnie burst into tears as she flung her arms around Beauty and was pleasantly surprised at the warm reception to her hug.

Remembering the scene now, Bonnie couldn't help her smile. It was hard to concentrate on studies when so much had happened in the last few days. Her thoughts were interrupted as the door opened and someone else entered the lecture room. No one was ever on time. She glanced at the figure who threw his bag down on the desk beside her and slouched into the chair. She looked again, and her mouth opened in shock at the familiar face smiling at her.

'Blaze! What are you doing here?'

'I'm taking a long overdue rest from work, remember?'

'But what are you doing here?'

'I came to see you.'

'But I'm in lectures!'

'So?'

The lecturer turned to see who was whispering. Immediately, Bonnie blushed and fell quiet while Blaze reached across the desk to take her hand.

'Sh. You're causing a distraction,' he whispered with a grin. Smiling back, she settled into her seat, enjoying the feel of Blaze's strong fingers wrapped around hers.

'He's a great lecturer!' Blaze said as they came out of the room into the bright sunshine when it had finally finished.

'He is?'

'You mean you weren't listening?' Blaze gave her a mock frown.

'Well, I have to admit it was a bit hard to concentrate with you sitting beside me.'

He grinned. 'Come on, Bonnie, I wasn't the distraction. You were the one whispering in class.'

'Well, I just had to know what was going on. It's not like you to suddenly turn up at uni when you're supposed to be at work.'

'I have a week off. I'm not supposed to be at work.'

'But what about the teenagers?' Bonnie couldn't help smiling at him.

'What about them?'

'Well, what if they have problems and you're gallivanting around the uni with your fiancée?' She blushed, even as she said it. The word fiancée still felt strange on her lips. It was a dream that had been shattered and she had put aside all hopes of ever belonging to this man again.

'Mr Mathison will be around.' Blaze's smile matched hers as he fiddled with the engagement ring on her finger. 'God can use him just as much as he can use me.'

At his words, Bonnie stopped and put her arms around his waist. 'I love you, Blaze Clements. I thank God for you every day!'

'Likewise.' His voice came out husky with emotion.

***

Though Bonnie had thought her wedding was cancelled, she soon came to realise that everyone else had believed it was merely on hold. For that reason, it wasn't hard to prepare. Her parents hadn't yet cancelled the booking for the reception and Mr Mathison had kept the church free, just in case. Flowers were still on order and invitations had been kept. The horse and carriage that had been arranged was still available.

'I want to keep our original date,' Blaze told her hopefully and she agreed. The sooner she married this man, the better.

'But I don't think Sky should live with us for the first year.'

Bonnie looked at him in surprise. That wasn't in the original plan.

'We need time together, to get to know each other without the responsibility of caring for a little one.'

'Blaze, I don't mind.'

'Maybe not,' he gave her a lop-sided grin, 'but I do. I want you to myself for a bit.'

***

Blaze's family arrived a week before the wedding and a delighted Beauty met each of them with an enthusiastic hug.

'What's that for?' her twin, Storm, asked gruffly. She laughed, knowing he was secretly pleased.

'Because I missed you.' She gave him a playful thump on the arm. 'And because you're my brother. Believe me, not every guy I come across gets a hug like that, so appreciate it!'

He stared at her, then broke into an uncharacteristic smile.

160

Beauty knew he didn't know what to make of her cheerful teasing It was a welcome change from the usual sarcasm and spiteful anger of her past.

'I hear you became a Christian,' Misty said.

'I did.' Beauty nodded. 'Who told you?'

'Blaze. He couldn't keep quiet about it!'

Beauty was about to respond when her father's bellowing voice interrupted all the greetings going on.

'Well, Blaze, I knew you could do it!' He beamed at his eldest son. 'Only you could make such a change in my little terror.'

All eyes turned to Beauty, while Blaze shook his head.

'I had nothing to do with it, believe me.'

'Yes, yes, I know you like to give all the glory to God, but I think you can take some of the credit just the same.'

'No,' Blaze assured him, 'if you want to give a human credit, give it to Beauty's friend, Chappy Eldwin.'

'Chappy?' Misty turned back to Beauty. 'Who is she?'

'He,' Beauty said. 'Chappy's nicknamed after Charlie Chaplin.'

Misty smiled knowingly and pulled her aside. 'Okay. Tell me about him.'

'Well, he's a good friend. 'He acts crazy and funny, but underneath, when you get to really know him, he's deep and caring. He's got a really good heart.'

'And you love him?'

Beauty stared at her older sister.

'It's okay.' Misty grinned. 'I saw the look in your eyes when you said his name. I know he's special to you. I've been through the same experience myself recently; falling in love and beginning to understand just what God's love really means. You can trust me with your secret.'

Beauty shook her head. 'It's not that I don't trust you.'

Beauty knew if she could trust anyone not to tease her about her feelings, it was Misty. The truth was, love had been so distant from Beauty's experience that the thought hadn't even crossed her mind.

Something stirred within her. 'Yes. I guess I do love Chappy,' she confessed, while Misty's dimpled smile deepened.

'I can't wait to meet him. Anyone who manages to make their way into your heart has to be pretty special!'

Beauty wasn't offended by Misty's blunt words. She was right. Her heart had been hard for so long she had forgotten what it meant to love. God had opened her eyes to true love and turned her heart of thunder into a heart able to feel and love again.

***

'I'm so scared I'm going to trip in these high heels.' Misty confided in Beauty. 'It's a long way down that aisle.'

Beauty gave Misty a quick hug. Both girls had been honoured when Bonnie asked them to be bridesmaids. Now, standing there in their beautiful dresses, they didn't feel quite so confident. Performing in the circus was a lot easier than this. At least their circus routine was practiced and familiar.

Beauty drew in a deep breath and tried to reassure Misty. 'You'll be fine. Just imagine you're still on Victorian Dream and you'll be right.'

Misty frowned and bit her lip. 'Beauty, has it ever occurred to you that it's strange the way I can ride a horse bareback and do all kinds of amazing stunts but I can't even walk straight without tripping?'

Beauty hesitated. Yes, it had. Often she had been the one to ridicule Misty for her clumsiness and despise her for her mistakes.

'Yes,' she finally admitted. 'And Blaze told me about how you fell asleep on the road. It scared me. I don't want to lose you.'

Misty came and put an arm around Beauty. 'It's okay. I haven't told Blaze yet, because this is his special day, but I'm getting it all looked into. The doctors think I have a medical condition that can be fixed.'

Beauty's eyes widened. 'Seriously? I never thought ...'

Misty smiled her sweet, dimpled smile. 'Me neither. Funny, I've lived with it all my life and never considered it could be something fixable.'

Beauty grinned. 'Yeah, a bit like me living in guilt. I needed to believe it was possible to be healed before I accepted the healing.'

'You look amazing,' Misty said as she looked at Beauty. Beauty smiled. She knew the blue of the dress brought out her dark complexion and hair in a way that was very becoming.

'So do you.' Beauty smiled, but stopped as Bonnie entered the room, now fully dressed in her wedding gown.

'Bonnie!' they both breathed at once.

'What?' She said. 'Something wrong?'

'No, something right!' Misty assured her. Bonnie's wide blue eyes held the radiant sparkle that Blaze had so cleverly captured in his portrait of her. There was no doubt he would think her beautiful today.

'I've just stopped worrying about people looking at me,' Beauty told her sincerely. 'I won't even be noticed!'

'Come on, you two!' Bonnie laughed. 'You're just saying that because you're supposed to.'

'I'm not!' Beauty pushed her in front of the mirror. 'Just look at yourself!'

Bonnie did. Her bright blue eyes were alive and sparkling. 'Alright,' she admitted. 'I look pretty happy. But why wouldn't I? I'm going to marry Blaze in less than an hour!'

The girls made their way gracefully to the horses waiting outside and Beauty felt a lump form in her throat. This was the first time she had been on a horse since losing Montford Express. The man Misty worked for had provided a horse for her. It was a beautiful, dark brown creature called Constant Shadow, but no horse could make up for her own white friend of fourteen years. Montford Express should have been here. If only …

She stopped herself. No time for regrets. God could bring

good from the most tragic of circumstances. Blaze and Bonnie's wedding was proof of that.

The procession of horses made their way to the front of the church and Beauty enjoyed the admiring looks. She stood beside Misty, waiting as Bonnie stepped down from the carriage.

Misty stood so close she could feel her shaking. 'I'm scared.'

Beauty squeezed her arm. 'Don't be. If you trip, I'll make sure I do, too.'

Misty chuckled. 'You will not!'

'I will. I promise!'

***

Beauty waited at the door of the church as music began to play. Chappy was ushering people in and raised his eyebrows when he saw her. He gave her a quick wink before continuing with his job. She grinned.

Blaze stood at the front of the church with his brothers by his side. Prince stood tall and regal, while Storm fussed over his bow tie. Beauty knew that if anyone but Blaze had asked Storm to wear such a silly thing, he would have flatly refused. He ran a hand roughly through his thick hair, causing it to stand on end more than ever, then glanced to where his father and sister, Starre, sat in the front row. Starre was shaking her head disapprovingly as he undid the top button on his shirt. Stubbornly, he looked away. Beauty grinned, knowing they would just have to take Storm as he came. No amount of fussing or head shaking from Starre was going to make any difference.

The music built up and all eyes turned to the door. Slowly, little Sky made her way to the front, grasping at her flowers and concentrating on walking the way Bonnie had showed her. Bonnie, the woman her Uncle Blaze promised would someday be her new mother. Sky would do anything for her.

Beauty glanced to her other brother, Prince. He stood

watching Sky with a stoic expression on his handsome face. What must he be thinking and feeling, knowing this was his own daughter, the one he abandoned? Was he too afraid to accept her? Did he feel any kind of guilt? If so, she felt sorry for him. She would begin praying for him; that he would come to know and accept God's love the way she had so that he could be set free from any guilt.

'Only Dad, Prince and Storm don't believe now.' She shook her head. Time to walk down the aisle. But her thoughts were still on her brothers and father. Did they think Christianity was a girl thing? No, surely they couldn't think that. Blaze was one of the strongest, most manly men she knew, and he had believed first.

She was aware people were smiling as they looked at her and she smiled back. This day was about Bonnie and Blaze and the miracle of their love. She would focus on them and worry about her brothers later.

Beauty reached the front and turned to watch Misty walk down the aisle without a hitch. She looked nimble and elegant and no one would ever guess how clumsy she could really be. Then came Bonnie. Blaze and Bonnie gazed at one another as the distance between them disappeared. Taking one another's hands, they turned to face the minister with nothing less than joy showing in their faces. Blaze, tall and dark, and Bonnie, once burned and heartbroken but filled with an inner beauty which drew all attention away from her scars.

Beauty allowed the tears of joy to run unchecked down her cheeks. If God could sort out the messes she had made in life, he could do anything!

Chapter Twenty Five

Beauty wandered around the reception hall feeling self-conscious and lost. She thought about going out to admire the magnificent horse she had ridden to the wedding. She also wanted to spend some time with Misty's horse, Victorian Dream. She missed Montford Express terribly, and had found comfort in seeing Misty's horse. And she had to admit that Constant Shadow was one of the most amazing horses she had ever seen.

'I don't belong in here, anyway,' Beauty told herself, glancing around at all the people in the hall. She moved toward the door but was stopped by a hand on her arm.

'Can I dance with you?' It was Chappy standing there, a smile on his pleasant face.

Shyness washed over her, but she managed to nod. 'Yes.'

He reached out his hand. Tentatively, she took it, thinking he looked handsome dressed in his usher's suit. She had watched him at the wedding ceremony, admiring the way he so spontaneously smiled at people as they arrived, then efficiently led them to their seats in the church.

'I don't really know how to dance,' she admitted as he now led her onto the floor where the bridal waltz was being played.

'I don't believe that. We danced at the disco, remember?'

'I mean, not this kind of dancing.'

'I'll teach you.' He smiled as he put an arm around her and drew her closer. 'I saw you ride in on that horse and I think you could do anything with that nimble body of yours.'

She caught her breath and willed her beating heart to still. His moves were smooth and graceful as he danced expertly around the floor, seemingly oblivious to her mistakes. Finally they came to a stop, but he didn't relinquish his hold on her. 'You look fetching in that blue dress.'

Her smile lit up her face, though she looked away shyly.

'I think you should take up ballroom dancing. I need a new partner.'

Her eyes flew to his in surprise.

'Would you?' he pressed.

'I don't know.'

He ignored her hesitancy. 'I need you. I can't think of anyone else I could put up with as my partner.'

'Put up with?' She caught herself, realising the light, teasing tone in her voice made her sound like Bonnie Blake.

'Okay, not put up with.' He smiled at her flaming cheeks. 'I could put up with several people, but I wouldn't enjoy it as much as dancing with you.'

Beauty swallowed, a lump seeming to get stuck in her throat. Chappy lifted her chin, gazing directly into her eyes again. 'Will you? Please?'

She could only nod, and his look was delighted. 'Thank you.

She hadn't realised how breathless she was until Chappy led her from the dance floor to a seat. She looked up and caught Misty's eye. Misty was grinning and Beauty bit back her own smile, turning to Chappy. 'I just remembered. My sister wants to meet you.'

Chappy chuckled. 'Which one? Everyone I meet here today seems to be your brother or sister.'

Beauty smiled. 'There are six of us.'

'Six? And you're all twins or triplets?'

'No. I'm a twin. The guy I was partnering today, Storm, is my twin. Prince and Misty – the other groomsman and bridesmaid – and Starre are triplets. Only Blaze is single.'

Chappy laughed heartily at her description of Blaze. 'He's the least single person I know in this room today. Now me? I'm a true description of single, even though I've been tempted to change that lately.'

Beauty blushed. What was he implying? Trying to hide her red face, she took Chappy by the hand and led him over to Misty.

'Misty, this is the friend I was telling you about, Chappy Eldwin.' Her words tumbled over one another as she moved to withdraw her hand from Chappy's. He tightened his hold and didn't let go. Misty looked down at their joined hands, then back to them with a knowing smile.

'Pleased to meet you, Chappy.' Misty's dimples moved in and out as she studied the young man before her. Beauty studied him, too, wondering what her sister saw. He had a small mouth, but one given to smiling. His sparkling eyes made him seem alive and Beauty knew then that he was more than special to her. Perhaps she did love him. She had certainly grown very fond of him.

'I suppose you're glad to meet Beauty's family at last.'

Misty had no way of knowing Beauty had insisted on being called Amy for the last year. Distinctly uncomfortable, Beauty glanced sideways at him and saw he was looking at her with meaning, though he spoke to Misty.

'Yes, although there is a lot about Beauty and her family I am yet to find out.'

She bit her lip, realising he had called her Beauty for the first time since she had slapped him for it.

'You didn't know about us?' Misty pretended to be horrified.

'Not until today.' Chappy turned to Beauty and his eyes looked deep into hers in something close to a challenge. 'But I intend to find out more about you all from this day on. Even if I have to drag information from you!'

Beauty smiled, swallowing hard. There was something different about how Chappy was treating her today. It was as though she were special to him. Her thoughts were confirmed when he put out an arm and drew her to his side before kissing the top of her head. 'I look forward to getting to know you better,' he whispered into her ear.

Chapter Twenty Six

Bonnie knew she would never forget a moment of her wedding day. She would never forget the way Blaze looked, nor the way he looked at her. She couldn't believe she could be so loved.

Once they were alone, Blaze put his hands either side of her face and gazed into her eyes. 'I can't promise I won't make mistakes and hurt you again.'

His tone was full of regret, but Bonnie merely smiled as she hugged him.

He still looked concerned. 'I want to be the perfect husband, but I'm scared about how much I'm going to let you down.'

'It's okay, Blaze.' She wrapped her arms around his neck. 'What we went through to get to this point was really hard, but it did teach me that it's possible to get through things like that. With God, we are always growing and changing for the better.'

Blaze was silent for a few moments before releasing a deep sigh. 'You're right. Whatever happens, there is always God's forgiveness just waiting to cover the mistakes I will undoubtedly make.'

'Don't forget I'm not perfect either,' Bonnie said, chuckling at his serious look.

'What?' He pretended to look shocked by the revelation.

She shrugged, giving him a cheeky grin. 'I forgot to pack my toothbrush for our honeymoon.'

He put on a look of horror. 'Right, that's it.' He turned toward the door. 'This is just too much.'

Bonnie caught his arms, laughing, and he drew her up into them. In all seriousness, Bonnie could not think of a place in the world she would rather be right now.

He spoke down into her hair. 'I just wish my brothers and sisters could find the happiness I have.'

Bonnie smiled up at him tenderly. 'If we keep praying I believe they will. But until they live completely for God, they can't know this kind of joy.'

***

Beauty was glad to have Starre and Storm staying with her while Blaze and Bonnie were on their honeymoon. She listened as they argued over breakfast and she smiled. She had missed them, and yes, she had even missed the conflict.

'You could have worn the tie just for the ceremony, Storm!' Starre's tone was disgusted.

Storm banged his plate of toast down on the table. 'Why?'

Starre gave her 'older sister' sigh. 'Out of respect for Bonnie and Blaze.'

'I didn't hear them complain about how I looked.'

'No, because they were so wrapped up in each other they didn't notice anybody else.'

Storm let out a triumphant laugh. 'Exactly! Because they understand that it doesn't matter how you look. Life isn't a performance, it's about who you are inside. Didn't you listen to that preacher at the wedding? Life is all about relationships.'

Beauty's brows flew up in surprise. Storm had been listening to Mr Mathison's message? Maybe there was hope for her brother after all. She ventured from her room and glanced at the two of them. 'I'll be back in about an hour. Just going to dancing practice with Chappy.'

Both nodded before recommencing their argument. Beauty shook her head and made her way out the door.

Chappy was waiting for her outside the town hall and his face lit into a smile at the sight of her.

'Ready?' He took her hand and led her inside.

Beauty glanced around the ball room, feeling awkward and unsure. 'I'm so nervous.'

Chappy gave her hand a reassuring squeeze. 'You'll do fine.'

She glanced down at her clothes. 'It feels wrong to be wearing everyday clothes and doing ballroom dancing.' She had been surprised when Chappy told her to wear whatever she wanted.

'We only wear full dress if we're performing,' he explained.

'Like the circus,' she said, and seeing Chappy's confused look, went on to explain. 'We practised in every day clothes, but we always dressed up for performances.'

Now Chappy was gazing down at her and she was concerned. 'Am I too sloppy?'

'No, you look beautiful.'

Beauty's dark eyes darted to his. She was surprised to see he was sincere.

He let out a chuckle as he led her onto the dance floor, his eyes full of wonder. 'To tell you the truth, I feel like the Beast with Beauty.'

She laughed, then sobered. 'Beauty is my real name – the name on my birth certificate.'

He smiled. 'I know. I asked Blaze. And it suits you. Do you mind if I use it?'

Beauty shook her head. 'No. I want you to.'

'And my real name is Hunter.' He lifted her hand to his shoulder and moved closer. 'Hunter Luke Eldwin. Before we get better acquainted, I want you to know that.'

'Hunter,' she said, trying out the name. 'I like it.'

He smiled. 'I like the way you say it.'

The music began and Beauty felt her fears fade away. All she could think of was the young man leading her around the dance floor, one hand holding hers, the other around her waist. Hunter Luke Eldwin; she loved him. And she loved the way God had reached into her angry heart and set her free – free to love.

ALREADY AVAILABLE FROM JENNY GLAZEBROOK

Book 1 Aussie Sky Series

Release 2014

Bonnie's world is happy and carefree until Blaze Clements and his horse-crazy family arrive from the circus. Is believing in God the only way to make sense of the tragedy that strikes?

Coming soon from Jenny Glazebrook

Clouds of Prayer
Book 3 Aussie Sky Series
Release 2015
Prince Clements captured Rachel's heart the moment he left the circus and rode into her school. But she is a minister's daughter and Prince has no time for God.

Mist of the Morning
Book 4 Aussie Sky Series
Release 2015
Roy can't work out if clumsy Misty Clements is clever and manipulative or if she is just as lost in the world as she seems. What is she hiding from him?

AUSSIE SKY SERIES BY JENNY GLAZEBROOK

Jenny Glazebrook writes inspirational fiction for young adults and is now publishing her Aussie Sky Series. This series includes six novels about a lovable ex-circus family and the lives they touch. Each novel focuses on a different member of the unusual, horse-crazy Clements family, their struggle to fit into everyday Aussie life and their relationship with God. *Blaze in the Storm* was a finalist in the CALEB unpublished manuscript competition for faith inspired writing.

More details about Jenny's books can be found on her website: www.jennyglazebrook.com